The Tygrine Cat

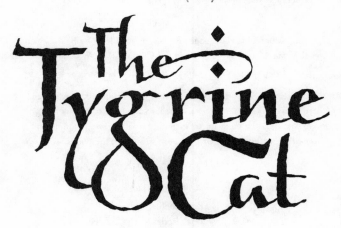

INBALI ISERLES

CANDLEWICK PRESS
CAMBRIDGE, MASSACHUSETTS

Copyright © 2007 by Inbali Iserles

Excerpt from "Honorable Cat" (page vii) copyright © 1972 by Paul Gallico and Mathemata AG, used by permission of Gillon Aitken Associates Ltd.

Map (pages viii–ix) drawn by David Atkinson

First U.S. edition 2008

Library of Congress Cataloging-in-Publication Data

Iserles, Inbali.

The Tygrine Cat / Inbali Iserles. — 1st U.S. ed.

p.   cm.

Summary: Lost and alone, Mati seeks acceptance from a pack of feral cats at Cressida Lock, but in order to defeat the assassin on his trail, Mati must unlock the secret of his true identity and learn to harness an ancient and deadly feline power.

ISBN 978-0-7636-3798-9

[1. Cats—Fiction. 2. Fantasy—Fiction.]   I. Title.

PZ7.I7742Tyg 2008

[Fic]—dc22   2007034213

2 4 6 8 10 9 7 5 3 1

Printed in the United States of America

This book was typeset in Weiss.

Candlewick Press
2067 Massachusetts Avenue
Cambridge, Massachusetts 02140

visit us at www.candlewick.com

For my parents

I am Cat.
I am honorable.
I have pride.
I have dignity.
And I have memory.
For I am older than you.
I am older than your Gods.

Paul Gallico, "Honorable Cat"

Far Bank

Weeping Willow

Boarded-up Church

CRESSIDA MARKET

Cherry Trees

Craft Stalls

Deserted Stalls

Entrance to Catacombs & Sparrow's Chamber

Fishmonger's Stall

Terraces

Pangur's Favorite Stall

Jess's Stall

UPSTREAM

Perimeter of Cressida Cats' Territory

Fishmonger's House

Prologue

The last glimmer of sunset settles over the desert. Black waves break against the ship, froth streaking the bow. Crouching in the cargo hatch, the Queen of the Tygrine Cats tastes the air. Her whiskers bristle. It is time.

She pulls away from her son. "I will never be far from you. Look to the setting sun, and you will find me," she tells him. The Queen turns, runs from the ship, sprinting along the gangplank and down onto the harbor.

Confused, her son calls after her. The engine groans, drowning out his cries.

Under her breath, the Queen chants a forgetting spell. Soon she will be far from his mind. Soon he will scarcely remember his own name. It is for the best.

A low mist clings to the harbor, masking the moon. With it comes a pungent smell like rotten eggs. Dark shapes shift among the distant pines, drawing closer. They have come.

"I am the Queen of the Abyssinia Tygrine. I do not fear death," she says.

Yellow eyes emerge from the gloom. "Then come— embrace it!"

The Queen shudders. She knows that voice; she knows those eyes. It is the cat they call Mithos the Destroyer, loyal to the Suzerain and his empire in the north. Standing behind Mithos, stepping out from the fog, is the army of the Sa Mau. Perhaps fifty cats, perhaps five thousand, long-limbed and lean.

The Queen watches them steadily. "So many of you, just for me?" she asks. Her words are answered by wailing gulls, which circle over the harbor. Their cries momentarily confuse her. They sound like the cries of a lost kitten.

"Not for you: for your magic. For your tricks," growls Mithos, with no hint of respect for the doomed Queen. Mithos serves only the Suzerain.

The Queen looks into his eyes. She sees many ages of the moon. She sees bitterness without boundary, untiring malice. She glances over her shoulder at the retreating ship. Her son is safe. It has not been in vain.

The soldiers of the Sa stalk toward her, shoulder to shoulder, flashing their fangs, poised for battle.

But the Queen addresses them as old friends. "Long ago, the Tygrine and the Sa ruled side by side, in peace. Can that time not come again?" Her golden eyes widen, and light seems to flow from them.

The soldiers of the Sa hesitate. Unsheathed claws falter.

"Fools!" hisses Mithos. "This is sorcery! Can you not see how she casts her spell over you? The time of the Tygrine is over! Long live the Suzerain! Long live the Sa!"

"Long live the Suzerain! Long live the Sa!" echo the soldiers. They surge out of the shadows, an endless stream of fighters, like termites from the husk of a tree.

The Tygrine Queen makes no move to run. "Mati . . ." she murmurs.

Even the gulls are still.

The first Pillar

A Stranger in the Marketplace

Over and over again, the sun wrestled the moon for dominance of the earth, a ritual dividing night from day. When Mati first became aware of this struggle, his was a floating home of shrieking gulls and furious surf. Soon the cries of the gulls faded and the ocean mellowed. Its purr was Mati's lullaby, the creaking of the ship's planks his morning chorus. Until today. On this morning, Mati awoke to unfamiliar sounds: the thumping of heavy crates being lifted onto the deck, voices barking directions, the strains and beats of an unknown song. Deep within the bowels of the ship, the engine groaned. The small ruddy-brown cat stretched for a few moments, then snapped to attention. Perhaps he had finally arrived—but where?

It seemed an eternity since Mati had first been nudged into the cargo hatch of the ship in the harbor of his old home. He recalled his mother's words: "Where the ship draws to land, there you must leave it. Until then, stay safe and don't let yourself be seen."

"And what then, Amma, what then?"

"Then, my son, you will be truly alone, free to follow your senses, to carve out a new life in a very different world. Let the three pillars be your guide."

He was only a catling, barely out of kittenhood, and memories of his life before the voyage were smudged like the ink of an old book. He had survived the long days on the ship undetected, stealing scraps. Indeed, Mati considered himself a master thief. He prided himself on his stealth. On a mission to the kitchen or the small dining room where the crew sat for meals, Mati imagined himself invisible, his narrow body hugging the dark cabin walls, dissolving into shadow.

Mati had found it easy to make his way around the ship unnoticed. There were numerous gaps between crate and corridor through which a stowaway cat could scramble. He could even squat under a chair only tail lengths away from crew members, realizing that these furless giants could smell him no more than they could a ghost.

Thirst was easy to quench. Mati had soon discovered the shower cubicle, where the drizzle of a faulty showerhead ensured that he could drink his fill once the crew was up and about the ship. But one trip above deck was enough for the catling, terrified by the impossible expanse of ocean and the salty air that stiffened his whiskers and stung his eyes. His territory was the world below deck, with its satisfying odor of the crew's rubber boots, oil, and leather.

On this morning, as unfamiliar sounds and smells alerted him to a change in the world, Mati froze in the cargo hatch and listened to the fading murmur of the ship's engine. Whiskers bristling with excitement, he pounced onto a ledge and out of the cargo hatch until, neck craned, he was peering into a damp autumn morning. Even in this dull light, his eyes ached as they adapted. A hazy sun was rising over looming gray buildings.

Mati's lips parted and his nose crinkled. He could taste the moisture in the air and knew that the ship had finally moored in fresh water.

After weeks on the ship and remembering almost nothing from his previous life, Mati was overwhelmed by a sudden fear. This would be his first opportunity to leave the ship, but his surroundings looked so strange. He missed the real home he could hardly remember and the mother he loved. What would she have advised?

He remembered again what she had told him before withdrawing from the ship: "Where the ship draws to land, there you must leave it."

Glancing about, Mati noted that the vessel had moored at a dock, on which men were preparing a small crane to lift the cargo onto dry land. He crept toward the left side of the deck, hiding between some pipes. Nearby, a gangplank had just been laid, and Mati was about to run down it when he saw two pairs of boots rushing toward him. Oblivious to Mati, the men marched up the gangplank, dragging a trolley behind them. Mati glanced back between the pipes to find the deck now blocked by a huge crate, which crew members were fastening to the crane.

"What are you doing?" demanded one of the men pulling the trolley.

Mati glanced up guiltily before realizing that the question was directed at one of the crew members handling the crate.

"B-crates off first—you will find these are the rules. White cottons, in style Oxford."

"I don't care about the style. They ain't coming off that way."

"Sir, I have my instructions!"

"Just back up, back up."

"B-crates first, please."

"Back up, will you, or we'll be here all day!"

"It's on the Instructions for Carriage. I have here copy, if you like to inspect. It specifically say—"

"Listen, you're in England now, and you might like to show a bit of common sense—"

"There is absolutely no need for . . ."

Although Mati understood human chatter, he scarcely had a sense of what the men were arguing about. He was busy making furious calculations. The men had not yet noticed him hiding between the pipes, but he had better leave quickly with this argument looming above his head. He dashed under the trolley on the gangplank. From here he judged that he was quite close to land, perhaps only two or three tail lengths away if he leaped at an angle from the gangplank. After a moment's deliberation, Mati crept out from under the trolley. He drew himself together, took a deep breath, and cleared the stretch with a running jump. He landed gracelessly and scrambled away from the ship, zigzagging along the ground with lurching steps. He collapsed under a pile of plastic chairs beside the dockers' yard. Nearby, men in overalls smoked cigarettes and drank milky tea from foam cups. Mati realized that a life on the ship had taught him how to keep his balance on the shifting seas but had ill equipped him for land. It took him a few moments to adjust.

Mati turned back to bid farewell to the ship, then hastened along the dock past warehouses and wastelands of concrete, following the river upstream. He passed lonely fishermen dotted along the riverbank and hurried beneath bridges that trembled under traffic. Finally he came to a small park flanked by peeling metal railings. He spotted the bare feet of an old man asleep on a bench. The man clutched a mottled blanket, a skinny dog with a rope for a collar asleep on the grass beside him. Mati hesitated, then backed away from the park and skirted around it until he saw stalls where goods were being exchanged for metal discs and pieces of paper. He spotted fabrics, sparkling silver trinkets, wooden objects, and all manner of curiosities. This must have been a popular spot with the humans; Mati noted a growing crowd clucking over the wares on display.

Pressed down low to the ground, the soft fur of his belly almost stroking the tarmac, Mati slunk under people's legs to investigate the marketplace. He lost his fears completely when he spotted a pigeon pecking about in the dust, a bird with a body almost as large as his own but a head scarcely bigger than his muzzle. Mati ran toward it, but the bird saw him coming and fluttered away noisily in a gust of grime and feathers.

"Ah! Come on!" cried Mati. "Come back! Please come back! I won't hurt you!"

Suddenly his nostrils filled with the smell of cooking meat. Seized with intense hunger, Mati followed his nose to a stall selling a collection of savory meals. A line of people snaked around one side. Along the other, Mati noticed a piece of spiced chicken that had fallen beside the bins. He made an excited dash for it, licking his lips in anticipation.

"And who do you think *you* are?" hissed a voice. Mati froze in his tracks. Three pairs of slanted green eyes were staring at him.

The Riddle
of the Bank

"**W**hat do you think you're doing on our strip?" snapped the first cat, a young silver tabby with pale green eyes. His two companions edged closer: a smaller silver tabby and a stout black-and-white with a stubby tail.

"Nothing," said Mati with alarm.

The first tabby narrowed his eyes. "Well, who are you? Where are you from?"

The young cats watched Mati silently for a few moments. They took in his shimmering russet coat. He stood on slender, fine-boned legs, and his tapering tail was tipped with black ghost-tabby stripes, so faint they were almost invisible. A golden M highlighted Mati's forehead, meeting an upside-down V. He stared at the catlings with unblinking amber eyes, rimmed in black and encircled by a band of cream.

The smaller tabby leaned over to the black-and-white and whispered. "Strange . . ." Mati thought he heard her say. "Different . . ." Her ears were pressed down flat and her whiskers inched forward. The black-and-white tilted his head to hear her, watching Mati steadily all the time.

Mati's first instinct was to turn and run. He glanced back at the crowds of people now bustling around the marketplace and thought that he could quickly lose himself in the throng. His nose picked up odors both delicious and unfamiliar: of bacon sizzling nearby, of hot dogs swimming in onion, and of burgers frying over fire. With a strange shiver, he absorbed the rich flavors of mackerel, cigarette smoke, and scorched rubber. The marketplace seemed vast—perhaps it spanned half the earth—promising a meal around every clutch of stalls. There would be other scraps of chicken, other opportunities for thieving if he escaped these strangers.

On the other hand, the catlings were clearly local, and a dark suspicion warned Mati that adult cats would not be far away. Against the sizzling meats, sticky-sweet perfume, and miserable stench of the bins, Mati's nose detected another scent. Fainter, but no less pungent, was the indisputable smell of a local tomcat. There was no telling how big or mean this ruling tom might be, nor the range of his chiefdom. Did his territory span the stall where hot dogs swam in the juice of onions? Would anywhere be safe?

Mati also realized that he was tired, that he had not eaten

since the last sunset, that he knew no one and had nobody to watch out for him. Considering what he had learned from his senses, Mati decided to negotiate with the strangers. At least they were only catlings; they couldn't be much older than him.

He cleared his throat. "My name's Mati. I just got here this morning after a long journey. I come from the other end of the ocean where days are hot and dry and nights are freezing cold, and I should probably just go home, but I haven't a clue where that is anymore, or how I'd get back there. And even if I could return, I don't think I'm supposed to . . ." Mati trailed off. He had meant to dazzle the strangers with his wit and charm, but he felt too miserable to know where to begin. His black-tipped, ghost-tabby tail curled around his flank.

The larger of the silver tabbies yawned noisily. He stalked up to the scrap of chicken that Mati had intended to eat for breakfast. The tabby wolfed it instantly, without offering a bite to the others, and licked his lips with a self-satisfied smirk.

The stocky black-and-white took a step toward Mati. He looked like a little harlequin, with half his face black, the other half white, and an all-black nose. Mati liked the look of him.

"You a normal cat?" asked the black-and-white.

Mati hardly knew how to answer that question, so instead

he said, "I had no idea that this marketplace belonged to anyone. I'm sorry about trying to eat your food. If you could just show me the nearest path out of here, I'll be going." He tried to address this to all of them, although it seemed that the larger of the tabbies was the leader.

"Get lost, stranger!" hissed the larger tabby, his sneer revealing small, sharp fangs. "You're not welcome here."

Mati's ears flattened close to his head, and he swallowed a distressed mew. He set his teeth. No, he wouldn't let them see him upset. He started to back away.

"Wait," said the black-and-white. "Maybe it would be OK for you to stay, but we'd have to check with Pangur."

"You crazy?" hissed the larger tabby. "Look at him. He's weird. He wouldn't fit in. Let him find somewhere else to stay. Let him try the Kanks! Hanratty'll know what to do with him!"

"He looks a bit like a rabbit. . . . Didn't Hanratty kill a rabbit once?" giggled the smaller tabby. Both silver tabbies hissed conspiratorially, as if sharing the funniest joke in the world.

"Don't mind them," said the friendly black-and-white. "They've never even seen a rabbit!"

"Have too!" cried the smaller tabby.

"Well, my fur's called an 'agouti coat,'" said Mati hesitantly. He wanted them to know that he was perfectly normal but realized from their reactions that his words had only added to their entertainment.

12

Rapidly gaining confidence, the younger tabby strutted in front of the other catlings, smoothing the fur behind her ear with a paw. "Ooh, look at me! I'm agouti!" At this, both she and the larger tabby collapsed laughing.

"Come on, fella, don't look so worried!" said the black-and-white. He skipped up eagerly to the stranger and gave him a shy smile. "My name's Domino. Those two are Ria and Binjax." He nodded toward the silver tabbies.

"Look at him! He's a freak," scowled Binjax, the larger silver tabby. Ria averted her eyes in apparent disgust. Her initial fear of the newcomer was dissolving into something altogether more hostile.

"Come on. He seems OK," said Domino, his zebra tail rising amiably.

Binjax glowered. "Anyway, Pangur won't let him stay," he warned. "He'll squish the impostor with his mighty paw!" This he illustrated with an excited leap and bat of the paw—"SPLAT!"

Mati's ears flattened in alarm.

Ria nodded and pounced in the air for good effect. "He's right," she agreed. "Pangur hates outsiders. He'll never allow a catling in without an adult to introduce him, and our parents are hardly likely to do that. Remember the cat from upstream?" The tabbies were closer now, almost as close as Domino, and Mati had taken another step backward without even noticing.

"A different situation entirely," declared Domino, but the

dilemma clearly had him vexed. He paused to scratch his head with a stout white paw. "We need to find a grown-up who'd be prepared to speak up for you before the kin," he told Mati, frowning.

"I should go," murmured Mati.

Suddenly, Domino beamed a great toothy grin. "We'll take you to Sparrow!" he exclaimed triumphantly.

An involuntary growl escaped Binjax's throat but he said nothing.

Domino led the way, his tail raised high. Mati followed close behind him, dodging humans clustered around the now bustling stalls. The silver tabbies trailed at a distance, refusing to acknowledge Mati's presence.

"Stick close to me, fella!" said Domino. He slunk under a large stall selling exotic pipes and ceramic pots. "Watch out for feet!" he advised. The young cats dashed toward a steep set of steps, leaping down each one—somewhat clumsily— until they were at the heart of the marketplace.

"Careful, there's an oolf over there!" hissed Ria. A mangy dog with a wiry coat and horrid jaws was ambling at its owner's heel, sniffing the ground, the leather leash slack at the human's side. Domino scrambled, narrowly avoiding the beast. The four young cats sharply changed course, but not before the dog caught a whiff of their scent. Its head snapped up, its eyes bulged, and it licked its lips. The catlings made a break through the crowds before the dog could spot them. It gave a yelp and strained on the leash, almost bringing its master to the ground.

"Bad dog!" he reprimanded, yanking it back.

The group had arrived at a lower section of the riverbank, past an imposing contraption consisting of cables, levers, and solid metal gates that seemed to pin back the river. Generations of graffiti, meaningless to cats, decorated the nearest side of the aged metal frame. The turbulent river pressed against the far side of the gates, threatening to break through. The pressure forced angry spurts of water to surge out of chinks where the two gates met.

The marketplace was now some distance away, and the nearest human was almost out of earshot. A couple of weathered, narrow boats tugged feebly against their moorings, nothing like the cargo ship on which Mati had arrived. The bank was given over to a thicket of weeds and unruly grass. Beyond it Mati glimpsed a steep drop to the water's edge. For a moment, the rising wind flattened the tangle of grass, and Mati noticed a dislodged pebble tumble into the swirling waters below. With a shudder, he turned back to Domino.

The harlequin catling began to enter the grassy verge nose first.

"Where are you going?" asked Mati, wide-eyed. He knew that the bank ended sharply not far beyond the grassy verge, where the river began.

"Just follow me."

"But the river!"

Domino blinked back at him. "Don't worry, fella," he said in a mischievous voice. "Sometimes you just have to take a leap of faith!" at which he dived into the grass and disappeared from sight. Ria followed without sparing Mati a glance, tail raised high.

Bringing up the rear, Binjax shoved past Mati. He paused and looked back. "Go home, stranger. You're out of your depth!" With a smirk, he leaped into the thick grass.

Mati sniffed the air, whiskers bristling. He tapped the grass with a tentative paw, but it gave him no clue as to where the others had gone. What had happened to them? The grass could not have covered more than a couple of tail lengths of bank, yet the catlings had bounded into it with such confidence. Could they be flailing in the water? Or had they played a trick on him? Perhaps Domino was in with the others after all and was only pretending to be friendly.

He waited a moment. He tried to remember what his mother had told him about such tricky situations. Instead he recalled her teachings on "the pillars" of a kitten's education: "A cat's instincts are the mainstay of his survival. These are the first pillar. But without judgment, these instincts may lead to ruin. Judgment is the second pillar."

Mati didn't know what this meant. And what was the third pillar? He knew there had to be a third—there was always a third. Perhaps it would be helpful?

He was still pondering the riddle of the bank when he heard scuffling several tail lengths behind him. Spinning around, he saw that the dog from the market had broken free of its owner and was bounding toward him, jaws foaming. The beast barked fearsomely as it bulldozed through shoppers, the leather leash flicking at its side like a snake.

Mati panicked. What had Domino said? "Sometimes you just have to take a leap of faith!"

The dog closed in: ragged claws, snapping teeth, putrid breath. Without a second glance, Mati dived through the grass and over the edge of the bank.

Mithos
the Destroyer

Mithos saw sand mountains extending across the desert. The jagged contours of a city pierced the skyline. Burger bars and pizza parlors jostled for space between high-rise apartment blocks. The road leading to the city of Zagazig was gridlocked with traffic. Motorbikes crisscrossed between cars; buses grumbled impatiently, bumper to bumper. Inside the buses, eager tourists flicked through digital photographs of pyramids, taken earlier that morning on the long road to the Nile Delta.

Mithos entered Zagazig enshrouded in shadow, slinking across roads and dodging wailing cars, down steps stinking of dogs and rotten fish. He was hunting for the secluded entrance that would lead him to his master. He wound along a familiar alleyway, over discarded soda cans, french-fry cartons, and cigarette butts, until he spied the sign of the red paw of the Sa Mau above a disused ventilation shaft. He gave a quick glance around to make sure that no one was watching. Even as he approached the opening, the sounds of the city dissolved behind him.

Mithos crept through the shaft for several tail lengths until he reached a low vestibule. Here he left the modern world behind; wordlessly, he slipped into the Suzerain's secret palace. The palace beyond the ventilator shaft had stayed the same for thousands of years, years that had seen the collapse of the ancient city of Bubastis and the rise of Zagazig, now a noisy metropolis. The palace remained, resisting the fast-changing world that clamored against its walls. Around it, buildings had been built and destroyed, electricity pylons had been erected, empires rose and fell. Yet none of this affected the palace or its occupants.

Mithos passed sentinels who shuddered in silent recognition, through a dank stone passageway illuminated by flames. Unannounced but expected, he drew toward the inner chamber of his master, the Suzerain.

Twin pillars, carved with images of scorpions and snakes, marked the entrance to the chamber. Suspended above the pillars was a sculpture of a rearing cobra, ready to spit poison at the Suzerain's enemies. A solitary eye at the center of the cobra's head glared down at all who entered.

Mithos passed under the serpent's eye and lowered himself onto the stone floor. Before him on a platform, his master sat frozen like a statue, a ghostly silhouette in a room lit only by a single candle. Crouched in the shadows, high priests chanted spells in the ancient tongue, under the unblinking gaze of the Keepers of Sa, the Suzerain's loyal bodyguards. Without instruction, the Keepers of Sa left the chamber. Still chanting, the high priests hurried after them, leaving Mithos alone with his master. Their mysterious incantations evaporated into the darkness.

"Most Majestic Excellency, son of the moon and master of the sun, your command has been obeyed: the Tygrine Queen is dead," said Mithos with head bowed.

There was a long pause in which silence swelled to fill the empty chamber. And then, his voice trembling with a rage he was struggling to control, the Suzerain spoke. "The spirits told me she is dead but another lives. He is the last, and he alone prevents me from taking what is rightfully mine."

"Another?" gasped Mithos. "There can't be . . ."

"You question the spirits?"

"No, my lord. Forgive me." Mithos bowed deeper, the fur of his brow brushing against the stone floor.

The Suzerain continued, "We who have been vigilant these long years lost the power of our senses, failed to recognize the betrayal happening before our eyes: in darkness, in secret, a forbidden child. A sedicia, living by crumbs of sun, drinking from the dew, flowering under rocks. Waiting for the western wind that will scatter its seeds across the bitter earth. Yes, Mithos. I, too, missed the signs. I have been deceived."

"A *sedicia*?"

"A wildflower, a banished flower. At the end, the Tygrine Queen was weak from many battles, prepared for defeat. Now she is gone, but I sense a strange new power. Can you not feel it, Mithos? It hovers outside my reach like a low flame. Given air, given space to grow, it may become dangerous."

"I do not understand, O Great Majesty," said Mithos, frowning.

"The Tygrine Queen defied me! I feel her son's body slipping away from me even as his spirit lingers."

"The Queen had a child? A Tygrine heir?" murmured Mithos in disbelief.

"Do you understand what this means? We have almost succeeded in realizing our noble purpose. All cats will be liberated from the shackles of human influence and placed under the Sa's command. The army of the Sa Mau will soon be ready to march beyond the borders of my empire, to declare one law across the earth. The Tygrine could ruin everything!" howled the Suzerain. He breathed deeply, and when he spoke again his voice was soft, almost as though speaking to a child. "Son of Mith, you will hunt down this sedicia, this heir to the Tygrine throne. My spies have told of his escape. By the powers of Sa, you must find him."

"And then, O Master?" whispered Mithos, fangs glistening in the half-light.

"And then?" echoed the Suzerain. His dark eyes radiated a passionate fury, but his voice was mild, almost regretful. "Then, Mithos, you must do what you do best. Destroy him."

Kippers
with Sparrow

Mati plunged several tail lengths before landing on a shallow ledge, just above river level. Heart racing, surprised to find himself alive and well and, more than anything, still dry, he peered over the ledge. Murky water swirled beneath him, lapping against the dilapidated brickwork of the bank. The stench of the river rose in acrid waves to sting his nostrils and prickle his eyes. Mati squinted against the water but could not see through it—an oily film gave the river a tarlike appearance. His distorted reflection danced across the surface, but the other catlings were nowhere to be seen.

With a shudder, Mati drew back from the edge. Above him, in the distance, he could hear the faint buzz of the market, and over it the frenzied barking of the wiry dog.

Mati realized that he was balanced on a ledge that could not be seen from the bank above. He turned to the brick-work and saw a narrow circular passageway, apparently built into the bank itself. Domino and the others must have entered here. It would be easy enough for them to scramble through, but a grown cat would struggle.

Where could such a tunnel lead? Mati wondered.

He entered cautiously, whiskers first. With tentative steps, he began to feel his way through the darkness. His heart thumped and his eyes widened. The shallow gleam from the bank brought dull shape to the tunnel walls. Soon, the dog's barking had faded away. Mati was left with the sound of the muffled padding of his paws and his hot breath in the moist air.

Eventually, the passage forked and Mati paused.

"At last!" came a voice. "I was beginning to think we'd lost you to that oolf!" Suddenly, through the shadows, Mati could see the white side of Domino's face.

With enormous relief, Mati hastened toward him in the right fork of the tunnel. He was about to thank Domino, to tell him about the leap of faith, to mention the pillars of a kitten's education and the dog's terrible fangs, but the black-and-white cat immediately turned and disap-peared down the tunnel, the white of his zebra tail glowing like the halo of a street lamp.

"Hurry!" called Domino. "It's better before high lunch." His excited voice echoed down the passageway.

What's better? thought Mati. The fur began to rise on the back of his neck involuntarily so that he had to coax it down.

Domino bounded ahead.

His paws have pressed against the floor of this tunnel many times; he knows exactly where we are and where we're going, thought Mati, envying Domino's confidence. For a moment he remembered the familiar smell of rubber boots and leather from the ship. Mati's senses fumbled their way around the new odors of the tunnel, drawing shapes from smells. He sensed the numerous pawprints of cats who had walked this path before him, the pattern of their coats, their distinctive saliva. If he concentrated, he could almost distinguish their murmurs of contentment. Fainter yet, something melancholy and restless of the long-departed cats hung in the still air. Unlike Domino, Mati trod carefully.

As Mati followed Domino deeper into the tunnels, he wondered where the tabbies had gone. He sensed that they were close, with their sneering faces and cruel jibes. If only they would give him a chance to show that he was ordinary. Why on earth had he mentioned his agouti coat? That had been a mistake, highlighting his difference. Mati suspected the trick was to fade into the background, to seem like the other cats. But how could he disguise his amber eyes, his long limbs, his black-tipped tail? He suddenly loathed these features. He admired Domino's broad, honest face and stout limbs.

After a while, the passageway forked again, this time branching into three more tunnels. Without hesitation, Domino took the middle road, with Mati close behind. After only several moments they encountered another fork, and Domino took the left of two tunnels. It became so dark that it was almost impossible to see anything, and Mati's other senses took over. Ears pricked up, he followed Domino's footsteps.

The two young cats walked briskly in silence. Soon the passage widened and was again illuminated by a faint light, this time ahead of them. Mati's heart quickened when he realized they had nearly arrived, that soon he would meet the grown-up cats—the one Domino called Sparrow and, worse, the one Binjax had mentioned—Pangur, was it?

Who is this Pangur and what did he do to the cat from upstream? Tear him to shreds? Drown him in the river? Make a pelt of his fur? Lost in such disturbing thoughts, Mati didn't notice the light growing brighter until Domino stopped.

"We're here," whispered the black-and-white, standing before what appeared to be an entrance to a chamber. "Now, don't worry. We'll just tell him that you're lost, that you came from far away."

Mati nodded. He blinked up and saw that the light was pouring in through a grating. Two tail lengths in front of them hung a circular wooden door, warped with age. The door was slightly ajar. Ria and Binjax were sitting under the grating, tabby markings crosshatched with stripes of light, clots of shadow collecting around their eyes, their smirks ghoulish. "Domino, are you sure . . . ?" Mati's voice faltered.

Ria and Binjax sniggered.

That's it, Mati thought. *From now on I've got to be tough. No cat is going to laugh at me. No cat!* He seethed quietly and his whiskers twitched slightly, but he remained silent.

"Come on," said Domino, ushering Mati toward the entrance of the chamber, oblivious to the hostility crackling between Mati and the tabbies. Domino walked right up to the entrance and meowed his presence.

After several moments, a husky voice came from the chamber. "And who might that be, to wake a hardworking *felis* from his slumber, I wonder?"

Mati's ears flattened in alarm. He had assumed that with a name like *Sparrow* their host would be a small cat, but no pygmy could be master of that voice!

"It's me, Mr. Sparrow, Domino. Ria and Binjax, too. And we have a visitor." Domino replied without making any moves to enter the chamber.

"Domino, you say?" said Sparrow. "Ah . . . Trillion's boy. Ye-e-es. Domino. And how is Trillion, young Domino? I trust she is still mousing, as ever?"

"Oh, yes, sir."

"And you are joined by Ria and Binjy? The children of Sinestra and Kroof?"

Binjax's ears flicked back and Mati swallowed a chuckle. "Yes, Mr. Sparrow sir, *Binjax* and Ria," Binjax corrected. Like

27

the other catlings, he stood stock-still, upright and respect-ful in the presence of Sparrow's voice.

"How is Sinestra, kits?"

"Our amma is very well. She had a slight cold earlier in the season, but it has passed and she's feeling much the bet-ter," replied Binjax politely, clearly making an effort with his grammar and pronunciation.

"And your father, Kroof—still finding odds and ends from the market?"

"Yeah," giggled Ria. Binjax gave his sister a disapproving swipe to the ear.

Another pause followed. Mati was beginning to suspect that Sparrow had fallen asleep when finally he spoke again. "So, young Domino, you said you had a visitor with you."

"Yes, sir. A catling named Mati."

Sparrow grunted. "A catling, you say? Mati, you say? Not from the market, then, not one of ours, you mean?"

"No, Mr. Sparrow, sir, but a good sort and something of a mouser, I think." This was a lie—both because Domino could not possibly have known what sort of hunter Mati was, and because had he cared to ask he would have discov-ered that Mati had never caught a mouse in his life. But Sparrow merely gave a long and thoughtful "Hmmm." Mati found this an odd sort of pantomime, with Sparrow on one side of the entrance and the catlings seated on the other. Nevertheless, he waited to be addressed, following the lead of the other catlings and resolving to speak only when spoken to. He glanced at Domino, who offered a reassuring blink.

"Well, then, kits, I suppose you had all better come inside for kippers."

At such an invitation, Domino clawed open the door at the entrance to the chamber and the catlings followed him down the two shallow steps that led inside. Sparrow, a huge ginger cat with small round ears, a broad face, and a saggy belly, was stretched across one side of the warm chamber on a patchwork of feathers and towels. Low pools of light gathered through the grille by the entrance. The chamber was surprisingly large and comfortable, with redbrick walls and an iron dome.

Sparrow struggled to sit up for a few moments, and as he dragged himself into a position fit to receive visitors, a confetti of feathers rose with him to swirl around the chamber, landing at the catlings' feet. With a great orange paw, Sparrow nudged a pile of kippers toward his visitors. "Eat! Eat!" he said encouragingly.

Mati could hardly contain his excitement. Out of politeness he waited for one of the others to take the first bite. Several agonizing moments passed in which Mati could think of nothing else before Binjax helped himself to a kipper. Mati fell upon the food with gusto. It was all he could do to chew before swallowing.

Sparrow chuckled heartily and readjusted himself among his plumes. "Ah, catlings!" he said. "What an honor, what a great honor. I rarely get visitors these days. Of course, there's that nice lady from the denim stall who brings me my supper, and meetings at the abandoned warehouse, but . . ." He trailed off as he took in Mati's appearance. He squinted slightly, Mati noticed, but only with his left eye. "You, kit. What did you say your name was?"

"Mati, sir. My name is Mati."

"Hmm. Come closer, Mati, let me have a proper look at you."

Mati approached the great ginger cat nervously.

Sparrow leaned forward and cocked his head. "My dear boy, you have a remarkable coat."

"Thank you," said Mati. Noticing the disdainful glances of the tabbies, he thought better of elaborating on its agouti quality.

"And your facial markings . . . like a tabby's, but where are the stripes? Quite extraordinary." Sparrow squinted at Mati intently. "Where did you say you were from?"

"He came up with the rubbish when they dredged the river," hissed Binjax under his breath. Ria snorted. Sparrow ignored them both and waited for Mati to speak.

Mati cleared his throat. "Well, Mr. Sparrow, I don't recall the name of my territory. It's hot there, much hotter than here, and I think it must be far away, as the sun rose and the moon set many times during my journey by water, in a huge ship that traveled to a dock. I followed the river a long way from the dock until I reached the park." There was so little that came to him clearly. He concentrated a moment and suddenly recalled the parting words of his mother.

"My darling, my kitten. You must now travel far from me, from the land that has loved you, and from the amma who gave you life. Perhaps one day you will understand why I have had to do this, what it means for an amma to lose her only child. But do not ask me to explain. You will leave, my dearest son, and realize your destiny. And one day we will be reunited: if not in this life, then in the next."

"But Amma, why must I go?" Hadn't his mother been a young cat? Her face against the indigo sky had looked so tired.

Only her eyes were bright as she hushed his questions with a tilt of the head. "There is no more time." She had stared at him sadly before turning toward the sea.

He remembered now. She had led the way to the harbor, ushered him onto a moored ship, crossed the gangplank alongside him, and nudged him into the cargo hatch.

Mati's mother had washed his head with rapid, confident strokes. "Wasn't it only yesterday that I could still carry you by the scruff? You have grown so quickly. . . ."

"Where am I going, Amma?"

"Far away, my child."

"Won't you come, too?"

"I cannot leave this place. My fortune is bound to it. One day you will understand. Look at me."

Mati had felt angry and frightened, had wanted to turn

31

away, but it was impossible to refuse his mother's voice. He remembered how her black-rimmed amber eyes seemed to radiate light.

"Where the ship draws to land, there you must leave it. Until then, stay safe, and do not let yourself be seen."

"And what then, Amma, what then?"

"Then, my son, you will be truly alone, free to follow your senses, free to carve out a new life in a very different world. Let the three pillars be your guide. . . ."

"Amma, please don't leave me!"

"I will never be far from you. Look to the setting sun and you will find me."

"Amma, wait!"

But she had sprinted down the gangplank, retreating into darkness before the ship pulled away from the harbor.

Mati's tail drooped when he recalled this scene, and deep in his chest was an ache impossible to explain. Looking up he found Sparrow and the catlings watching him expectantly. He did not have the will to talk about his mother, so he said nothing of this memory and was relieved when Sparrow spoke.

"Now, tell me Mati, have you ever 'owned'?"

Mati understood that Sparrow was referring to the strange but ancient custom of cohabitation between feline and human, whereby a feline lived alongside an educated human, a "hind," and came to "own" them, in a manner of speaking. The "owner" would offer comfort and protection to the human, who in return would provide regular food and stable lodgings, a practice cats referred to as "socage." Mati seemed to remember something about such arrangements but had never himself granted socage. "I don't think I've ever 'owned,' sir. I don't dislike hinds, but I can't remember ever having had to look after one."

"Ah, good," said Sparrow. "And I will tell you why. Sit, young Mati, do, and I will—or have the, that is . . . the kits have probably explained: we are a kin, that is, a group of feral cats. Do you understand what that means?"

Mati shook his head. In truth, it was difficult to follow Sparrow, as his sentences took more turns than the tunnels leading to his chamber.

"Well, I am probably not the best *felis* to explain this to you, but it basically means that we do not own hinds. It is not, as you say, that we dislike them. We live alongside them well enough in the marketplace—well, that is to say, most of the time. No, rather it is that we like to do things our own way around here, and ownership is an unwelcome burden.

"Our kin was set up in Olden Times. Relations between the ferals and the hinds have not always been so smooth. It is said that our ancestors were persecuted horribly—hunted, tortured, drowned, and burned. This I learned even in my kittenhood, but never why. It is said that we were feared and hated in equal measure before the hinds made their peace with us, and the nature of hinds has always been to destroy

33

what they don't understand. Which is a great deal, I'm afraid to say.

"Urban house cats escaped the tyranny of the hinds and formed cat-only communities. They scorned the Ancient Ways, the rights of socage and ownership, and it is told that some even whispered of a time before the hinds, when our people walked the earth proud, wild, and free. . . . But I digress—and what would a humble market cat know of such matters . . . ?" Sparrow trailed off. His squinty eye settled with agitation on his twitching tail. With unusual speed and agility for a cat of his girth, he swiped at his own tail with a "Cease, you beast! Will you now stop it? Stop it!" until it was still. Sparrow turned his attention back to the catlings with a *pirrup*, a murmur of good humor, and seemed surprised to find they had edged away slightly and were watching him with concern. He resumed unperturbed.

"Now . . . where wasn't I? Oh, yes. These tyrannized cats yearned above all for freedom from the hinds. It was in such spirit that the Great Founders"—and here he gave a *pirrup* of respect—"the Courageous Ladies Wilhelmina and Moullier, Consorts of Freedom, initiated what has become our thriving community. Several of the cats hunt, like Domino's amma, Trillion, but most of us do well enough on food left by the market hinds. I have a lady from the denim stall who makes sure I'm kept in kippers." Sparrow chortled heartily and rubbed his belly. "Ye-e-es. Kippers . . . But where wasn't I?"

"You were telling Mati about our kin," said Ria helpfully.

"Yes, thank you. We live together here in the Territory, the vicinity of the marketplace, a fine location on the water, as it provides many sources of food and interest. We use the old drainage system as a network of passageways—it is said that this chamber in which we sit was once used to pump water, before the modern lock was built. Of course, there are dangers, and we must be careful, not least of oolfs and the nearby road."

Mati had no idea what Sparrow meant by the "road." Everyone shifted uncomfortably. Clearly it was a hazard too terrible to talk about.

Sparrow continued, "And some of the characters who visit the market are colorful, to say the least, but this freedom, this freedom and this community . . . that is to say, it is these things that make us special. None of us has ever 'owned' a hind—except for Jess, that is. Jess wears the collar."

"Jess is a *stray*," said Ria. She uttered the word in a low, disapproving voice. Clearly it was something very odd, but Mati thought better than to ask.

Sparrow changed the subject. "Well, then. Let us devise a method by which to introduce you to our little community. For this is doubtless why you came to a silly old cat like me." At this, Sparrow winked at Domino—or was it just his squinty eye?

Mati could not be sure. "Thank you, Mr. Sparrow," he said with genuine gratitude.

"That's all right, my lad. As luck would have it, tonight

will be a full moon. You kits can rest here and eat your fill, unless of course you are needed at home?" The catlings shook their heads. It was a busy market day, and they would not be expected for hours. "Good," said Sparrow. "In that case, do rest awhile. At the occasion of the full moon, the cats of the lock will convene for a starlit meeting, from which the presence of catlings is usually forbidden. You, young Mati, will be making a special appearance. But not yet . . . I might ask one of you kits to go and fetch the chicken leg my denim lady usually brings me right about this time. Indeed, by the sun tickling my whiskers, I'm reckoning it's lunchtime again. . . ."

The Cats of Cressida Lock

"**I** fear that pesky moon is climbing high above the cherry trees. Come, kits, time to go home. You must entrust Mati to my paws now," Sparrow sighed. It took him several moments to get up, and when he finally managed it, a feather from his nest floated into the air to rest on his low ginger brow, giving him a roosterlike appearance. None of the catlings dared tell him of this development, although Ria giggled.

At that moment, Mati was distracted by more pressing matters. He was wondering how a cat of Sparrow's size would make it out of the maze of narrow passageways under the marketplace. Instead, Sparrow led the way out of the far end of his chamber and through a door. Moments later, he and the four catlings were standing on a patchy tree-lined stretch of grass that ran along the far side of the market, upstream from the lock. Fortunately, Mati noted, the feather on Sparrow's brow had blown away.

It was a breezy night. Drifting clouds revealed occasional stars. The branches of the cherry trees swayed lazily under a high white moon. The edges of Mati's memory clawed toward another image, far away, or long ago. Of a night biting cold and squid-ink black, on which countless brilliant stars lit up a cloudless sky. His pulse raced. Was this a memory of home? He closed his eyes a moment to concentrate but the image had gone.

"See the big lock? Against the bank, that's where we entered," said Domino.

Mati glanced over at the contraption. He marveled at how far they had walked through the underground tunnels. He wanted to ask all sorts of questions but decided to save them for a better moment. In any event, his mind now turned to the full-moon meeting, and the thought set his fur on end.

"Do we *have* to go home, Mr. Sparrow?" whined Ria. She, like her brother Binjax, did not seem interested in Mati's welfare so much as curious.

"Do we, do we, do we?" asked Domino.

"Ah!" said Sparrow. "Now, let me see. What would your ammas say? Yes, I mean no, they would surely say a kitten must sleep, a kitten is not to attend. That's right, 'No kitten may attend the full-moon meeting.'"

"I am *not* a kitten," hissed Binjax under his breath, but Mati heard him. "And how about Mati?" he scoffed a little louder.

"Ah, but Mati must meet the other cats. Oh, no, a different matter altogether! Now, do make haste, young kits, your parents will flay me if they learn that I've kept you away!" said Sparrow as Binjax and Ria slunk away miserably.

Domino sidled up to Mati before leaving. "Good luck, fella! Show them your best!" He winked and ran to catch up with the others, zebra tail raised high. Mati was sorry to see him go.

"Now, cheer up there, lad," said Sparrow reassuringly. He meandered toward the marketplace with Mati at his side. Mati could already sense the presence of other cats. As they neared the far side of the deserted market square with its locked stalls, he spied a circle of them in the moonlight. Some sat up on stalls, others on the ground. At least one nestled in the branch of a tree.

Mati fought the urge to turn and run. He ordered himself to be brave but noted impatiently that his tail still clung to his flank. He commanded it to rise, but it ignored him.

The marketplace was deserted of humans. Some distance away, at the bins closest to the nearby park, an old man dressed in a tattered coat was foraging for food. His boots crunched over broken glass. His callused hands roamed through the bins, drawing out foam tubs with leftover noodles, potato chip bags, and half-eaten pizza. Yet farther away, traffic sighed on the road, and the muffled bass from a nightclub sank through the tarmac to tingle Mati's paws.

As Sparrow and Mati drew closer to the assembled cats,

Mati realized that the full-moon meeting was already in session. On a raised stall overlooking the marketplace, a wedge-faced Siamese was talking with a nasal voice. "And I know some of you will say, let summer come and then we can address the issue, but I say, be prepared," he droned. "We know that the rats are capable of seizing our homes, taking over our food sources by simple force of numbers—"

"A rat is no match for us!" called out a cat from the audience.

"Maybe not, but what about thirty rats? Or fifty? Remember that those vermin multiply tenfold in the time it takes for a cat to groom his coat."

There were nods and murmurs of agreement.

Sparrow leaned over to Mati. "That's Fink the Sagacious, Warden and Rat Catcher," he whispered. "A perfectly nice fellow, but he does go on so." Sparrow grunted impatiently. "Let the rats come," he muttered to no one in particular. "What I can't protect of my own fine stash of food is not fit for any cat's consumption."

A black tom leaped onto the stall next to Fink. His velvety coat gleamed in the moonlight, his powerful tail swished as he addressed the gathering, and vivid streaks of his musky odor fanned out around him on the evening breeze like an invisible cloak. Even before he spoke, Mati was in no doubt that this was the alpha tom, the one whose scent he had detected earlier in the day. This was the head of the kin.

"And that, of course, is our leader, *Pirrup:* the Courageous Chief Pangur, Lord of the Realm. That is his correct title, but don't worry about using it; you can call him Pangur," whispered Sparrow. This last comment came as a huge relief to Mati, who found the title complicated and its word order peculiar. He had already tried and failed to memorize Fink's proper title.

"Thank you, Fink, for drawing the matter to our attention," said Pangur. "Let us readdress the matter when the daffodils are in bloom along the riverbank. All in favor?"

A chorus of meows echoed among the assembled cats.

Pangur nodded. "And all against?"

This time, his words were met by silence.

"Good," said the handsome tomcat. "On to the next matter on tonight's agenda . . ."

And so the meeting continued, with cat after cat taking the stage. Mati caught Sparrow stifling a yawn.

Mati glanced again into the crowd. Suddenly, he noticed Domino, Ria, and Binjax peering above some shrubs on the verge of the deserted market. He quickly turned back to Pangur so that Sparrow would not follow his gaze.

"I trust there is no other business?" asked Pangur, glancing about the assembly. His question seemed to assume that the answer would be no. Mati looked at Sparrow, expecting him to speak, but the great ginger cat said nothing. "Good," said Pangur, tail swishing. "I thank you for your patience. And now, Cats of Cressida Lock, I draw this meeting to a close."

The audience started to stand up and shuffle about, smoothing back whiskers, clearing throats. Mati sensed the excitement rising from their fur. And then, in unison, they began to sing, a caterwaul the likes of which he had never heard before:

> *Brown rat, underbelly, filch and fly, dominion, chiefdom,*
>   *eye-for-eye*
> *Truth and vengeance, tit for tat*
> *When you take on a Cressida Cat!*
> *Stick together, hunt together, eat together, call together*
> *Sing together, purr together, fight together, fall together*
>
> *Socage, do we grant it? No! Ownership is for our foe!*
> *Independence from the hind*
> *Feline wisdom, feline mind*
> *Stick together, hunt together, eat together, call together*
> *Sing together, purr together, fight together, fall together*
>
> *Live forever.*

The cats' anthem concluded in whoops, mews, and prances. A young brown tabby scratched his forepaws against the cobbles; a small blue scraped her claws excitedly on a stall. Slowly, the assembled cats prepared to leave, pirruping and leaping. Sparrow, too, had been caught up in the high spirits, his deep satisfied purr contributing to the sounds of euphoria. Mati watched wide-eyed. Only the young black tom seemed composed as he glanced about his kin. Suddenly, his fierce eyes settled directly on Mati, who edged closer to Sparrow's huge flank.

"Ahem," began Sparrow. "Forgive me, *Pirrup*: the Courageous Chief Pangur, Lord of the Realm . . . well, yes, we—that is, I have some business."

Pangur eyed them keenly. "You might have said so before I closed the meeting."

"Quite so, f-f-forgive my poor etiquette," stammered Sparrow. He clearly wasn't used to this sort of thing.

"Please come and join me. Cats, your patience; the meeting is still in session." Members of the audience who had started to leave resumed their places with interest.

Sparrow padded reluctantly toward the high stall with Mati following close behind. The ginger cat clambered onto a lower platform with a sigh and made the final leap onto the podium with a great deal of effort, landing heavily. Mati heard tittering from the audience and felt angry and hurt on Sparrow's behalf. Sparrow, however, did not seem remotely fazed by it. "Come on, then," he said to Mati, who sprang up effortlessly to land at his side.

An immediate hush fell. Mati felt the wind rise slightly, pressing against his russet coat. Pangur remained on the stall in silence, his powerful tail swishing, his face expressionless.

Everything Sparrow did, he did slowly. Momentarily, he scratched his ear with his hind paw. He cleared his throat noisily. Finally, he said, "I would like to introduce everyone to Mati. This is Mati." He nodded toward the little ruddy cat. "Mati came to us on a boat, a big ship that stopped at a dock far beyond the Territory. He followed the river from the dock until he reached the marketplace. He is a curious young thing. He isn't sure where he's from, but he's a capable mouser. I'm sure we can put him to good use."

Mati was mortified that the mousing lie had now been spread like a bad rumor throughout the entire community, but he thought it too late to right the matter.

"He's a fine young fellow, prepared to work hard, and although he has no amma to speak of and no one to vouch for him, he seems to me a feline of the highest credentials," Sparrow went on. "So I would like to . . . that is, I ask you to consider the possibility of his joining our kin, that is, our community, being the Cats of Cressida Lock." With this, Sparrow finished. He licked his lips and sighed deeply.

"And why should we let him join?" snapped a tabby queen.

"Sinestra the Courageous, Defender of the Territory," whispered Sparrow. "Ria and Binjax's amma."

"Rather ragtag and bobtail if you ask me," added Fink, the Siamese cat, edging closer.

A beautiful white Persian leaped onto their stall and stood a short distance from Sparrow and Mati. "Good heavens, will you look at him!" Her nose wrinkled. "Are you sure he's one of ours? I mean, he looks rather"—she lowered her voice to a scandalized whisper—"*African wildcat,* if you know what I mean!"

"Arabella, that's quite absurd," said Sparrow amiably.

"No, I agree with Arabella—maybe he's one of those jungle cats I've heard about," said the whiny-voiced Fink, joining the Persian on the raised stall.

"Enough!" snapped Pangur. Fink and Arabella fled from the stall to resume their places in the gallery. "All this petty sniping is beneath us. Let us hear the catling."

"Yes," agreed a young tortoiseshell-and-white cat in the gallery. "Let Mati speak!"

"You would say that, *stray!*" growled Arabella, addressing her comment to the tortoiseshell-and-white. "Not a true Cressida Cat—not even an adult! What's she doing here, anyway?"

"Enough, I said!" hissed Pangur. He turned to Mati. "Come, now, what have you to say?" he coaxed.

Mati looked at Pangur, then to Sparrow, who gave him a reassuring smile.

"Well . . . Mr. Pangur the . . . the Courageous Chief of the . . . Chief of the Realm . . ." Mati stuttered—to an explosion of feline laughter. *Oh, most shaming of all possible blunders,* thought Mati, *to botch the chief's title.* His amber eyes widened.

"Just call me Pangur," said the kin leader.

Mati nodded deeply—to more titters from the gallery—and forced himself to continue, voice faltering. "I am very

45

grateful to you for allowing me to explain myself, Mr. Pangur. I came to the river by boat and arrived at your territory this morning. I think it is a very pretty marketplace. . . ." At this there were several murmurs of approval. "I have some education, and I remember the first two pillars of a kitten's instruction, although I can't remember the third. . . ."

Pangur looked at him blankly.

Perhaps the pillars aren't known at Cressida Lock, thought Mati, dropping the subject. "Well, I am not sure if I could be much help to your community, but I would certainly try. I can't really mouse"—at which disapproving whispers—"but I can steal and swim—well, in shallow water, and . . ."

Astonished gasps came from the gallery.

"What did you say?" asked Pangur in surprise.

"It's true, I've never really hunted mice," admitted Mati dejectedly, expecting the tomcat's wrath.

"No, no—about the swimming!" To his amazement, Mati thought he saw Pangur shudder with fear.

Mati blinked into the audience. For a moment, just a moment, stunned silence surrounded him. His whiskers bristled, and in those stolen seconds, time froze. He heard a hum rise beneath him, like a low, mysterious voice. He thought it spoke his name. Then it was gone. That feeling. And he was once more a small ruddy cat in an unfamiliar marketplace, surrounded by strangers and a long way from home.

"Mati . . . ?"

"Oh. Well, I would steer clear of anything as deep and dirty as that river, of course, but yes, I don't mind a swim occasionally, so perhaps fishing . . ."

Again, whispers rose from the gallery.

"Cats don't swim!" exclaimed Sinestra.

"We don't even like water!" agreed Arabella.

"More than a slight understatement," said Pangur quietly.

"Perhaps he's an otter!" suggested Fink.

"Or a sea squirrel!"

"Some kind of strange furred fish!"

"Don't be ridiculous!" snapped Pangur. "He's a cat. Mati is clearly a cat." He turned back to Mati. "Aren't you afraid?"

"No, sir, Mr. Pangur. Why would I be afraid?"

"How did you learn to swim?"

"I can't really remember," answered Mati. "I can't remember much. . . ."

"Were you a house cat?" asked Pangur.

"No, Mr. Pangur. I have never owned. I lived with my amma. She is the only one I remember. There were others, too, who took care of me when she was busy, but I can't really recall them."

"Busy?"

"Yes, sir." On reflection, Mati could not be sure what she had been busy with. His mother had rarely hunted, as there were other cats to do that for her. There was so much that Mati did not understand. Memories danced at the corners of his vision, fading even as he looked on them, slinking into shadow.

"I see," said Pangur, although it was clear that he did not really see at all. He was silent a moment. "I will permit you to stay here on a trial basis, and we shall reconsider the issue in the spring. In the meantime, I hope you will learn a little more about our community here at Cressida Lock."

"Oh, thank you, Mr. Pangur!" exclaimed Mati with relief. Sparrow smiled, but from the gallery Mati heard indignant hisses and tuts of disapproval.

"Well done, Mati!" whooped Domino from some distance, unable to contain his excitement.

"Domino!" snapped his mother, Trillion. "What are you doing here?"

Pangur came closer and whispered so that the other cats could not hear. "But be careful, Mati. There are members of our feral kin who will not agree with my decision and will seek to prove me wrong."

As Sparrow and Mati jumped off the platform, it was to the jeers of other cats.

"Outsider!"

"Go back where you came from!"

"Don't listen to them, young Mati," said Sparrow protectively. "They'll come around, and all will be right. You did well up there, my lad, and I, for one, think you'll be fine."

"Thank you," said Mati, trying to ignore the snipes and the caterwauls. *Everything will be all right*, he told himself. *I'm not so different from any of them; they'll soon learn to accept me as one of the kin.*

But with unease Mati remembered the deep aching hum that had made his paws tingle as he stood on the stall. And as he followed Sparrow away from the crowd, he had never missed his mother so much nor felt so alone.

Beyond the Empire of the Sa

Mithos knew a hundred tricks to make himself invisible. He could blend effortlessly into his environment, draw the prying eyes of passersby away from him, hide himself from life even as he wound his way through its midst. He was more a conjurer than a true sorcerer, a master of illusion rather than magic. Eyes that looked upon him could barely understand what they saw—instead they saw nothing.

His preference was for darkness, but now he sought to cover as much ground as possible, traveling by daylight, stopping rarely.

Mithos stole through cities and along railway tracks, across lonely deserts and waterways heaving with noisy motorboats. He entered olive groves and vineyards with tireless determination, powerful but light-footed, twigs barely cracking under his callused paws. Where he passed, thousands of starlings dozing in the high branches of cypress trees took to the air, stirring the heavens with the beating of their wings. Babies awoke, screaming before their bewildered parents. Windows edged free of their catches, flying open to let in a moist wind like stolen breath.

Mithos existed now for a single purpose: to follow the son of the Tygrine Queen to the edges of the earth and stop his heart in the name of the Sa. The task was by appointment of the Suzerain. Mithos could rely on his master's many allies to help him on his journey, although he acknowledged no need of them. The Suzerain's power extended far beyond the boundaries of his formal empire. Even now, secret wars were being fought and alliances forged, silently observed by the Sa's countless spies. Then there were the Suzerain's shalians, mystic cats who knew spells from the ancient world, summoning energy from rocks and magic from the moon.

The darkness that escaped from the Suzerain's eyes flowed like lava across rifts and mountains, sank under water and crossed continents. It drew before Mithos to clear him a path.

Lost

Early the next day while Sparrow slept, Mati padded out of the tunnels. He blinked into the misty morning, tasting it with his nose and whiskers even before he could see it with his eyes. "A cat's instincts are the mainstay of his survival," he remembered his mother telling him. This was the first pillar of a kitten's education.

Mati met no other cats on his travels. He paused at a jewelry stall, delighting in the attention paid to him by the owner and her customers. "Angel" and "darling" they called him, as they ruffled his fur and tickled him under the chin. He rewarded them with his throaty purr.

He picked up breakfast at a sandwich stand. The young market vendor was relaxing before the morning rush and spoiled Mati with chunks of bagel slathered with cream cheese. Feeling sated and happy, Mati bounded along the stalls and soon ran into several of the cats from the full-moon meeting of the previous night, including Sinestra, mother to the tabbies, and Arabella, the beautiful Persian queen with the snub nose and disapproving eyes. As he approached, he heard them whispering to one another.

"Something of an oddity . . ." muttered Arabella.

"Ways other than our own . . ." agreed Sinestra.

Another cat said something Mati didn't catch, but he knew it was bad when the others snorted in agreement.

None of the cats addressed Mati or looked directly at him. Although he was a stranger to the marketplace, he knew exactly what this meant—in the cat world, eye contact was reserved for the respected. Mati slunk past them, his ears flattened against his head, his tail trailing behind him like a fallen kite.

Mati thought of Domino, the friendly black-and-white who had stuck up for him even as the others jeered. He wondered what the catlings did during the day—whether they took lessons in hunting, history, and tradition, as he seemed to remember that he had, and where they played. Investigating the marketplace on his own was no fun anymore.

He climbed under a low stall and watched people's feet as they milled past. He liked the soft murmur of sneakers on the damp tarmac better than he cared for the staccato click of high heels. He was intrigued by the occasional whirr of bicycle wheels and impressed by the squelch of boots.

In the shadows, every swinging bag and arching foot

drew Mati's attention. Glass beads on a woman's handbag caught the sun and scattered it across the tarmac like showers of diamonds. Mati batted at escaping light with a ruddy brown paw. Perhaps this is why he failed to notice a low figure slinking in the shadows until it was a short distance away, peering at him under the far side of the stall.

The sensation of being watched struck Mati suddenly. With a howl he sprung around, claws unsheathed and fur on end. "I have fangs and claws, and I know how to use them!" he cried in a voice that he hoped was convincing.

"Don't be afraid," replied the stranger, a skinny tortoise-shell-and-white catling with a red collar at her throat. She carefully slid under the stall to sit a short distance from him, a small bell tinkling on her collar. Mati immediately relaxed at the sound of her voice. The queen began to wash herself. She was telling him that she wasn't a threat. But it also showed Mati she was nervous.

"Who are you?" he asked.

"My name is Jess. Perhaps you have heard them talk about me?"

The name sounded familiar, but Mati was not sure why. He said nothing and waited.

She continued, "I was at the full-moon meeting last night. I live here, among the kin. But I, like you, was not born into it. I am lost."

Of course! Jess was the one they called the stray. Mati could not be sure what this meant, but even in the darkness under the stall he became aware of two things. First, that Jess had a beautiful voice—smooth, low, genuine; and second, that she seemed sad in a way he could not understand.

"They don't like strangers here," said Jess. "I see how they treat you. But, remember they'd be like that to anyone they didn't know." She said this while still washing, without looking up. "They're out of touch here. I know that it's the feline way to entrust oneself to spirits and destiny, but this lot scarcely draw breath without a chant or a curse."

"Where I come from, it's said that a cat with a powerful spirit may return time and again in different bodies and different lives." Mati was quite surprised by his own words. He wondered for a moment where they had come from; distantly his mother's voice completed the sentence for him: "It is even said that the soul of a cat of exceptional nature can live forever."

"Is that so?" said Jess.

Mati nodded his head lightly and glanced at her. "I only arrived here yesterday. I guess you know that. I almost didn't get off the ship in the first place—these hinds were arguing about how to get the cargo off or something, and they—"

"You understand hinds?" demanded Jess, interrupting. Suddenly she was staring at Mati, watching him closely.

"Of course. When I listen. Doesn't everyone?" he replied, bewildered.

"But you've never owned?" persisted Jess.

"No," said Mati. He was starting to feel uncomfortable with her questions.

"How odd," said Jess. "The ferals can't, you know."

"Can't what?" asked Mati.

Jess's tail jerked impatiently. "They can't understand hinds. I can, I suppose because I lived as a house cat for most of my life. But I wonder how you've learned the knack."

"You owned?" asked Mati curiously, glancing out at passing shoppers.

"Yes. I owned the sweetest old hind," sighed Jess. She looked away. "Now I live by myself in the locked-up stall at the edge of the marketplace."

"I'm staying with Sparrow. He's been great," said Mati.

"Yes, he seems nice. Not bothered about what the others think, I suppose. Which is just as well, given what they say about him. . . ."

"What do they say?" Mati knew he sounded defensive. He was upset to think that the ferals would be cruel about Sparrow, who seemed so harmless.

"They say . . ." Jess hesitated.

"What? Go on!"

She watched Mati steadily, as if trying to decide what to tell him and what to hold back. "They say that he's old and lazy, that he's no kind of tom."

"No kind of tom? What does that mean?"

Jess shrugged. "It means that he's never had a queen, I suppose. It doesn't matter. They'll say anything, especially

56

Arabella and Fink. They say things about me, too."

Mati was torn between feeling upset on Sparrow's behalf, although he didn't fully understand what Jess meant, and curious about what they said of her. But he thought it was too rude to ask, and now Jess was crawling out from under the stall.

"Have you had the tour yet?" she asked.

"No. I've been into the tunnels, well, the bit where Sparrow lives, and that other end over by the lock, and walked around a bit."

"Would you like me to show you?"

"All right." He followed Jess cautiously. His instinct told him he could trust her, but he had only just met her, and he didn't want to let his guard down. Judgement, he recalled, was the second pillar of a kitten's education.

They walked and talked, keeping out of the way of humans.

"The catacombs—those tunnels running under the market-place—they're vast. Probably larger than you realize," Jess began. "I'm not really sure just how far they go, but they certainly reach the lock and, from there, the park, and I think they run right under the marketplace."

"And are all of them occupied?"

"By the Cressida Cats? Not all of them, I think. Some are too narrow to enter or have been filled with concrete, or are too close to sewers—infested with rats or crammed with rubbish. The rest are used by the Cressida Cats."

"When you say the Cressida Cats—"

"I mean the market cats."

"Are there others?"

"Other ferals? Not in the market. The Cressida Cats are powerful. Pangur is young but respected. But there are other kins, near enough. They're dangerous. They'd do anything to take over the market, and especially the catacombs, which give the kin an advantage. But they don't dare. I heard Trillion and Pangur talking about one in particular. They didn't know I was listening, but I was. I think they called him 'Hanratty.' He's some kind of neighboring kin leader. I reckon he leads the Kanks' kin. The Cressida Cats are always gossiping about the Kanks. Pangur seemed to know him."

Mati felt the fur on the back of his neck bristle and his tail instinctively puff up. Jess stopped. They had reached the towering elm where the full-moon meeting had taken place the night before. Most of the stalls at this section of the market were still deserted. Jess sprang up onto the closest one and looked back at Mati, meaning for him to follow her. He joined her on the stall and sat down, overlooking the marketplace.

"Not every day is a busy market day," said Jess. "Today isn't. You'll start to know when to expect the busy days. They're more fun, because there's more food, more entertainment, that sort of thing, but they're also dangerous, because there are hinds everywhere, and where there are hinds there are oolfs."

"We saw one yesterday."

"You and Sparrow?"

58

"No, actually. I met some catlings—Domino, Binjax, and Ria."

"Oh?" Jess was impossible to read.

"Yes, they were the first cats I bumped into. Domino took me to Sparrow."

"Did the others come?"

Mati glanced at her. It was his turn to hesitate. "They came, but they didn't help." There. That showed whose side he was on.

"They wouldn't," agreed Jess. "I don't really know about Domino, but those tabbies are bad news. Of course you don't have to take my word for it, but for what it's worth, I'd watch my back with them."

Mati nodded.

"Now, can you see that building with the tall sort of tower?"

Mati glanced out over the marketplace. He saw a small boarded-up church surrounded by craft stalls. A lower cobbled area formed a semicircle around the far side. Beyond, he knew, was the lock.

"You don't want to go much farther than that. There's a huge road that circles around this whole area, around the marketplace, on the far side of the park, and right up to the edge of the terraces upstream."

"What's a road?" asked Mati.

"An endless concrete pathway with huge machines that move quicker than any cat. The road's dangerous. Never go near it. Cats from this marketplace have died on that road. A young queen, not long before I arrived. Perhaps that's why they let me in, to make up numbers—who knows? I've heard of others. No one talks about it, but I think you should know. Those machines don't stop for anyone. You wouldn't stand a chance."

Mati shuddered.

Jess glanced at him with deep green eyes. "Let's walk."

Mati nodded. They jumped down and he followed her into the heart of the marketplace.

They wandered between stalls. "You hungry?" asked Jess.

"I had some food earlier, but I can always manage more," said Mati. All concerns about the road had vanished from his mind. He was watching a lanky woman in gigantic boots and a tight blue outfit brush back a matted knot of pink hair with the back of her hand.

"What do you fancy? Let me see. . . . There's Chinese chicken, Thai beef, hot dogs . . ."

"Fish!" exclaimed Mati.

Without even thinking about it, Jess and Mati had been drawn to the rich perfume of the fishmonger's stall at the center of the marketplace. It boasted a variety of shimmering morsels on ice: silvery sardines, red snappers, glistening pink prawns. The two young cats crouched under a bench some distance away and watched wide-eyed.

"I've never seen anything like it!" sighed Mati. He stepped forward but Jess called him back.

"We mustn't go a whisker closer. The fishmonger is a spiteful old man who never shares even a tailbone of his precious fish." Jess's voice was heavy with regret.

Only then did Mati become aware of the sinewy man towering over the stall. As far as Mati was concerned, no human was ugly or beautiful—they were just different. But the funny thing was, Mati realized, the fishmonger looked rather like a fish himself, with pale oily skin and a jaw that stuck out like a trout's. Even his eyes seemed to bulge in a fishy sort of way.

And as if to prove Jess's point, the man began to mutter angrily. "Disgusting animals, pests, vermin . . ."

Mati closed his eyes. He detected the presence of several felines, but his sense of smell told him they could be only kittens, catlings at most. They were close, probably just out of view, perhaps three or four of them. In a moment, he sensed their youthful spirits, their fearlessness, their inexperience—all the things that made them young. His whiskers bristled at their hunger and thirst for excitement. "I think it might be Domino and the tabbies," he said, turning to Jess.

She gave him a searching look, glancing back at the stall and again at Mati.

"Go on, get away from that snapper!" shouted the fishmonger. He grabbed a bucket of water and threw it across the left side of the stall. Ria, Binjax, and Domino bolted from the stall, their fur drenched. The fishmonger watched the retreating cats with satisfaction.

Without thinking, Mati ran toward the other side of the stall.

"Mati, wait!" cried Jess.

Mati sprang toward the stall, pounced up onto the netting on which the fish were displayed, and yanked it down with his claws, springing off and sprinting away with Jess bounding behind him. He glanced over his shoulder to see a hail of ice cubes and a couple of mackerel crash to the ground. He slowed down, trying to decide whether it was safe to stalk back to the stall.

"Thieves! Vermin!" cried the livid fishmonger, shaking his fists.

No, it wasn't safe, Mati decided. He thought of the mackerel with longing all the way back to the cherry trees, where the two young cats finally caught their breath.

Jess was watching him closely.

"He deserved it," offered Mati.

"Well, I wouldn't deny that," said Jess. "But don't expect the others to appreciate it—if they even noticed. And something else . . ." She paused.

"Yes?" asked Mati.

"It's only . . ." Jess started to wash herself. "It's really amazing, Mati. Before you ran to the fishmonger's stall, only moments before, your eyes seemed to light up. It was as if they were glowing! I've never seen anything like it in my life." She licked her paw.

"Really?" asked Mati.

"What were you thinking at the time?"

Mati thought for a moment. He had felt hungry, frustrated at the sight of food in such abundance. He had felt how unjust it was that there could be so much in existence and so little to feed his empty stomach. Suddenly he realized . . . but no, that would be too strange.

"What is it, Mati?" Jess was watching him again in that searching way she had.

"Even before I saw Binjax with the others, I was seeing the stall from *their* point of view. *It was as if I was one of them* . . . I just wanted to share in a little bite of fish, just a little . . ."

"But how did you even know it was them? You knew they were there before you saw them. . . ."

"I sensed them."

"That is no ordinary talent," said Jess with a look of awe.

"No?" Mati had no idea what other cats saw or felt. It had never occurred to him that his senses were different, only that he *looked* different, as everyone pointed out. The thought that he might *be* different worried him. He was already unpopular—the last thing he needed was to seem even stranger to the ferals.

"I feel as if I've met you before," said Jess.

Mati shrugged. He was quite sure that he'd never seen this young queen before in his life.

Jess narrowed her eyes and tilted her head. "I know that isn't possible, but . . . you look so familiar. Where have I seen you?"

Master of Thunder

The Suzerain was keen for news of his servant's progress. Outside, the sun bore down on the streets of Zagazig. Shaded in his secluded chamber, the Suzerain watched as high priests circled him chanting spells to protect Mithos on his mission.

This was not all he saw. For memory has its own eye and the Suzerain had lived many lives. He remembered when the desert had been divided into two great lands across life-giving water. He remembered the daughters of Te Bubas and their feuding dynasties. He remembered a time when his kind had been honored and feared by all.

The Suzerain sat upright, lowered his head, and closed his eyes. Thinking, not thinking. Calling the spirit Alia, willing the ancient powers . . . until from the east came the distant rumble of thunder. The Suzerain opened wide his black eyes and stared in a trance across the chamber. "I penetrate stone and metal, dissolve them to powder and water. I cast my sight into the darkness," he whispered.

Under the low chanting of the priests, the Suzerain suddenly heard the high-pitched buzzing of a single fly. The insect raised its metallic-blue body from the floor of the chamber and sought out the exit, under the archway of the rearing cobra, through the corridor illuminated by flames, into an early evening sky humming with a distant storm.

A Lesson
in Manners

"Let us begin again. Our leader is?"

"*Pirrup*: the Courageous Chief Pangur, Lord of the Realm."

"Well done, Mati. Now, how about a queen? Take Arabella, for instance. Say she earned herself a *Pirrup*."

"Well, then I suppose it would be *Pirrup*: the Courageous Arabella, Mistress of Hunts."

"No, no, no!" said Sparrow. He sighed and expertly spooned another morsel of fish into his mouth with a curved paw. As Mati had been at Cressida Lock for some time now, Sparrow had taken it upon himself to educate the catling. "Her correct title would be *Pirrup*: Arabella the Courageous, Mistress of Hunts. The word order is all-important."

"Rats! I'll never get the hang of this," said Mati.

"Yes, you will, my boy. Now, if Pangur was to take Arabella as his queen—"

Mati giggled. He found it hard to imagine Pangur with the prissy white Persian.

Sparrow continued, undeterred. "Which is unlikely, as you know—but anyway, if he does, then everything changes. Then you would be right about it being 'the Courageous Arabella,' but of course it would be 'the Courageous Lady Arabella.' 'The Courageous' and 'the Sagacious' always come after the name *except* in the case of leaders. If you keep that in mind, the rest is easy."

Mati was not convinced. It seemed so pointless.

"Just remember," Sparrow continued, "at the first kill or fight won, a suffix is added to the cat's name, intended to describe their calling."

"What's a suffix?" asked Mati.

"Good question! I suppose you would call it something following the name, just as your tail follows your body. So when you do finally catch a mouse, you can be known as 'Mati, Slayer of Mice,' or something to that effect. The honor is marked by a short ceremony at the following full-moon meeting."

Mati tried to pay attention, but his mind started drifting.

"At a later stage—and this is a fine rite of passage— where a cat has earned greater respect in the community from battles fought, hunts, or debates won, a second suffix is added at the end of the title. Either . . . ?"

"'Courageous' for a hunter or fighter, or 'Sagacious' for a thinker," offered Mati.

"Or anyone else to whom the community wants to pay respect but who isn't a hunter or fighter. Like 'Fink the Sagacious, Warden and Rat Catcher.' That said, I don't know that that lazybones has caught a rat in his life, but he can certainly talk, and you know what it's like with these things, fifty percent politics."

Mati nodded politely, though he wasn't sure what Sparrow meant. He wondered whether Sparrow himself had a title and, if so, what? He dared not ask, in case the answer was no.

"Now, you don't have to panic—proper names are only truly necessary on formal occasions. There was a time when these would include the full-moon meeting, but all that has changed. Pangur doesn't stand on ceremony. . . . And who can blame him? He's young, full of energy and ambition."

Mati thought about the striking black tom.

"Do you remember where the *'Pirrup'* comes in?" asked Sparrow. Mati frowned. His mind was all a-jumble. "No?" pressed Sparrow. Mati shook his head. "Very well," Sparrow went on. "The prefix *'Pirrup'* is reserved for the very highest-ranking members of the community. Most cats will never earn this honor. It is awarded only to a cat of the right status who does something amazing. Pangur earned his *'Pirrup'* on defeating the old chief in open combat. Trillion gained hers by entrapping a huge colony of mice during the great famine last winter, over the hind festivals when the market-place was vacant. We all of us feasted for days. . . ." Sparrow was lost in the sweet memories.

"Good morning, Mr. Sparrow," announced Domino from outside the chamber.

"Come in, come in!" said Sparrow.

"I was wondering if Mati would like to join me for a bit?" said Domino, hovering at the entrance. Mati smiled and turned to Sparrow.

"Well, now, young Domino, I was just in the process of schooling Mati in how to correctly address members of the community. . . ." Sparrow glanced at Mati, then back to Domino. Both catlings pleaded with their eyes. "But I suppose it is nothing that can't wait, and I daresay you've already had enough for now, haven't you, Mati?"

"Thank you!" exclaimed Mati and Domino. They said their good-byes and took the short exit to the cherry trees.

"Hurry up, Mati, I want to show you this amazing pile of fallen leaves over by the park!"

They scampered along the marketplace until they came to a gigantic mound of huge golden leaves. Swept into steep piles along the park verge, they awaited bagging and collection. To Mati, each leaf resembled the palm of an ancient human hand, slightly cupped and riddled with veins.

Mati heard a chirping from one of the bare trees that overhung the railings of the park.

"Look!" said Domino. He was watching the pretty bird that hopped among the branches, puffing its white bib and red breast in song.

"Let's get it!" said Mati, secretly knowing that the bird would fly away long before they could reach it.

Domino shot him a look. "You can't even joke about that. That's the first robin of the harvest moon!"

"What do you mean?"

"Don't you have that tradition where you come from?" asked Domino.

"What tradition? I've never even seen a bird like that before."

"Well, you'll see plenty of this one. It's always around here. It's good luck to lay eyes on the first robin of the harvest moon. This robin brings the first sign of a warm spring, even though winter is almost here. You know, it's like a . . . a symbol. Like it means hope and long, warm nights and good eating. But you can't *eat* it, ever! That's bad luck, *really* bad luck."

"Who says?"

"Everyone!" said Domino in disbelief. "Haven't you ever heard that? *Everyone* knows about the first robin of the harvest moon!"

"But what's a 'harvest moon'?" asked Mati.

Domino rolled his eyes. "It's the moon that marks the end of summer and the start of autumn." He shook his head, smiling. "I can see I'm going to have to teach you everything. Like this: look out!" He dived into a leaf mountain. Sycamore leaves shivered and rustled as he disappeared beneath them.

Mati leaped in after him, plunging into the light, crispy foliage. For a few seconds he sat in silence, surrounded by the rich colors of autumn, a fragile tapestry of gold and oxblood red. Then he said, "Bet you can't see me!"

"That's not fair—you're leaf colored; that's cheating!"

"I'm not leaf colored; the leaves are *my* color. They're copying *me*!"

"How do you figure that one?"

"Well, my color doesn't change, does it?"

"So?"

"The leaves looked down from way up there, and they were jealous, and they thought they'd come down here and steal my color!"

"You're bonkers!"

"I know," agreed Mati. He blew gently on a leaf right in front of his nose, which stirred slightly. As it did, he spotted the white tip of Domino's zebra tail. There was no way he could creep up on him silently. He would have to make a leap for it. "I suppose we're done then," he said quietly, giving the impression that he was farther away from Domino than he really was. "You'd never catch me, and I couldn't catch you—I mean, I reckon you'd be fast as a wildcat."

"I am," agreed Domino.

Mati pounced, caught the end of Domino's tail for a moment under his paw, and both of them were off in a flurry of flying leaves. Mati slammed into Domino's back when the harlequin catling stopped abruptly, tail puffed. Jess was standing in front of him.

"Don't creep up on people!" hissed Domino.

"I didn't; you ran out at me," said Jess indignantly. The small bell on her red collar tinkled.

Mati trotted up to her, breathless. "We were just . . ." Somehow he felt guilty. "Do you want to play?"

Domino glanced at him questioningly. "You know each other?"

"Jess gave me the tour."

"Really?"

Mati shifted uneasily. "We were . . . The idea is that you hide in the leaves and . . ." He glanced behind him. "Oh, dear . . ." Several of the leaf mountains had collapsed.

"I know another game," said Domino. "There's a runt oolf, hardly bigger than a cat, tied up on a leash near the old church. We can bait him—it's hilarious. He goes yip-yip!" Domino imitated the high-pitched bark enthusiastically. He started pawing the air. "There there, oolfie—BOOM!"

Jess watched but said nothing.

"What do you think?" Mati asked her.

"I think . . . I'll leave you boys to it." She turned away.

"Don't go!"

"She's busy, let her," said Domino. Jess flashed green eyes at him. "She'll spoil it—strays don't know how to play," he added quietly to Mati, who cringed. He knew that Jess had heard.

"Would your amma want you to bait the oolfie, I wonder?" asked Jess. Trillion had appeared in the distance and was strutting toward Domino, glaring.

"Oh perfect . . ." muttered Domino.

Trillion took in the scene. She glanced with disapproval from Mati to Jess. "Domino, what on earth is going on here?"

"We were just playing."

"It's time for your lessons."

"Later, Amma, please."

"No. Now."

"But we were about to . . . We were in the middle of a game."

"While you're still young enough to call me Amma, you don't play, you learn. When you're grown up, I won't care how you spend your time."

"But when I'm grown up, I won't want to play! I'll become boring like all grown-ups." He shot Mati a desperate look.

Trillion turned to leave. "That's not my concern. My concern is to see you schooled. Come *on*, Domino, this is not a matter for debate. Any more out of you, and I'll send you to the Kanks. Let Hanratty school you!"

At this threat, Domino gave up trying to convince his mother and started trailing miserably after her toward the catacombs.

"One day, a normal day, I got up with my hind and had my breakfast of soft boneless meat that comes in a tin. I stepped out of the cat-door, and played for a bit in the garden, crossed into another garden, then another, and then there was a road, and then . . . Then I couldn't remember where I'd come from . . . And the more I tried to get back, the farther away I seemed to be." Jess told Mati this without looking at him, daintily washing a tortoiseshell-and-white paw. "It wasn't so long ago that I had never met any other cats. I spent all my time with hinds. Mostly only one hind."

"Do you remember what sort of place you lived in? I don't even know how hinds live, not really," said Mati.

"We lived in a big house, and he used to talk to me a lot. Mainly it was just us. Sometimes his family would visit, and I liked his granddaughter, although she had this habit of brushing my fur the wrong way. His daughter was different. She didn't like cats, and she was always complaining.

"My hind was at home most of the time. I stayed in and looked after him during the day and only went out for a few hours at night so that he wouldn't wake up suddenly and miss me. He liked to have me around. He used to tell me about his work."

"What sort of work?"

"He had a special room. He called it his study. He read symbols splashed across bound paper—hinds are fond of those. He was always looking at sketches of buildings. Very old and beautiful buildings, he said. I'd sit with him. He told me everything. About how the hinds once had slaves and they forced them to build great shrines, places where the hinds worship their gods. All sorts of interesting stuff."

"What do you mean by 'gods'?" asked Mati.

"I'm not sure how to explain," replied Jess, frowning. "I suppose a 'god' is a sort of invisible chief who shows the hinds how to live. You know—what to eat, how to dress, that sort of thing. Hinds are forgetful and need to be told stuff like that."

"Are there lots of these gods?" asked Mati, wrinkling his nose.

"Yes, I think so. Well, I've never actually seen one, but that's the impression I got. My hind certainly mentioned a few. There were even hinds who worshipped cat gods once! That's what my hind told me, that in some places it was a crime to kill a cat, a crime punishable by death."

"Gosh!" said Mati.

"Yes. They're superstitious, too—not as much as cats, though."

"What do you mean?"

"Some of them believe in powerful forces that can't be explained. Oh, I don't know, that the weather is symbolic, that dreams mean something—"

"Dreams *do* mean something," Mati broke in. It was almost as if his mother had spoken through him. Surprised at his own interruption and slightly embarrassed, Mati urged Jess to continue. "So do all hinds believe that sort of thing, then?"

"Not all of them. Some of them don't believe in things they can't see, and as gods are invisible, they don't believe in them. There's a name that the hinds use for those people, but I forget it. The hinds quarrel about it among themselves."

"Really?" To a cat, the unexplained was a part of life and certainly a part of death. Mati wanted to know more about the strange things that humans got up to and their extraordinary beliefs—but suddenly Jess was rising to leave.

"I'll see you later," she said.

"Where are you going?" Mati was surprised by her abruptness.

"Nowhere in particular." She wandered away.

Mati watched her go. It seemed to him that sadness clung to her like a shadow.

The First Robin

Several days later, Sparrow and Mati were sitting alone underneath the cherry trees, peering out at the distant stalls. It was a sunny day, crisp and cold. Their breath floated before them as white mist. Two full moons had passed since Mati's arrival on the marketplace, and he was gradually becoming familiar with the ways of the ferals.

Mati still shuddered when he remembered how the others had mocked him at the full-moon meeting where he had been introduced. Many of the ferals still whispered about him when he passed them in the market square, and the tabby catlings maintained their open hostility.

"There's no market at next sunrise. Some of the ferals will gather here at twilight. It's a sort of tradition. Nothing much happens, just gossiping really," said Sparrow.

Mati's mind wandered to Jess. Would she come tonight? What was she doing now? Was she in the locked old stall, sitting alone? "Will you be going, Sparrow?"

"Not sure, boy. Now, there was a time when I would scarcely miss the opportunity for a chit-chattering. There were so many stories once! About bravery and cruelty, clever little kits with bright blue eyes, wicked hinds and fish dinners. . . . Where do you suppose they've all gone?"

Mati couldn't answer. Perhaps something happened to stories that were no longer repeated. They grew old, died alone without ceremony. Mati felt sure that he, too, had known stories once, in his scarcely remembered life before the ship. He felt a twinge of regret for all those lost fairy tales his mother must have told him when he was a kitten. Even now, he felt the shiver of their presence, like ghosts, without color or flesh. Just an echo of something magical of his first days, gone forever.

Sparrow glanced at Mati with his squinty eye. "Don't be sad, boy; we'll soon find new ones." Then his tone changed dramatically: "*Get out of here!*"

Mati jumped.

"Not you, boy!" A metallic-blue fly, a bluebottle, came to rest on Sparrow's brick-red nose. Sparrow froze. "Easy . . . *easy* . . ." The big ginger went slightly cross-eyed, brow furrowed. Suddenly he batted furiously at his nose, rolling on the tarmac. The bluebottle darted away.

"Rats! You almost had it, too!"

"Didn't I?" agreed Sparrow. He opened his mouth as if to say more on the matter but was distracted by shrill chirrups. "Ah! Speaking of stories, here's a good 'un! You see that bird up in the branches?"

Mati looked up. "The first robin of the harvest moon?"

"So you do know the story?"

"No, it's only something Domino said the other day about the bird being good luck. He didn't say why."

"Ah! Now I have a tale for you. Long, long ago, when the Great Founders of our kin, *Pirrup*: the Courageous Ladies Wilhelmina and Moullier, Consorts of Freedom, spent their first autumn at Cressida Lock, they had little by way of food. Lady Wilhelmina was a supremely good huntress—a tabby, you know—and . . . How does it go? Yes, I remember! Lady Wilhelmina was out stalking on the night of the harvest moon when she came across a robin. There are some who say it was in the park downstream, but I always like to believe it was just about here, near the cherry trees."

In the distance, Mati noticed Domino, Binjax, and Ria wandering among the stalls. He sighed and looked back at Sparrow.

"Lady Wilhelmina caught the little robin and was going to, you know"—Sparrow swiped the air with his paw, his eyes bulging and tongue hanging out—" do away with the small thing. The bird cried out not to kill it, that if the lady spared its life it would see to it that winter would be merciful, spring warm and easy, and food plentiful. Well, Lady

79

Wilhelmina didn't really believe the bird. There are those who'll say anything when their life's on the line, and why should she believe that a creature so small could have so much power? But Lady Moullier approached then, and she urged Lady Wilhelmina to let it go—not because she thought the good luck would be real, they say, but simply because she sensed the bird's fear and pitied it. Some say the Great Ladies didn't actually talk to the robin, that they couldn't have, that there's no talking to a thing so small and dumb, but I don't believe that. The mistress cats were full of the magic; they could talk to anyone or anything.

"Anyway, so the story goes, the bird flew away. And that winter was mild, spring was warm, and food was suddenly plentiful. And each year, it is said that the first robin seen at the harvest moon must be spared, and even our most powerful instinct—which would cause any one of us to gobble it up—must be quelled somehow, because no one is to kill the first robin. And to my almost certain knowledge, no one ever has."

Mati liked this story. He looked again to the small, red-breasted bird. It hopped from branch to branch briefly and took flight. Mati had never spared much thought for birds before but somehow it comforted him to know this tiny creature would be safe.

In his hidden palace in the city of Zagazig, the Suzerain stirred. He was in a trance, neither awake nor asleep.

"I feel him, Great Spirit Alia," said the Suzerain.

"They are close now," the spirit reassured him. "They are searching for him. They will find him."

The spirit's voice faded beneath the chants of the high priests:

Ha'atta, Ha'atta! Sa can see through
Harakar, Harakar, draw us to you
Draw us backward, draw us inward
Darkness, Harakar, chaos, Harakar
Ha'atta, Ha'atta . . .

"I cannot see him," said the Suzerain.

"Have patience, my lord. The forces of Sa are potent."

"Can you see him, Alia?"

"I can. He knows nothing. He is young, weak."

"I sense him, Alia."

"Soon you will know him as I do, my lord. They are very close. The thunder is coming. Soon the sky will weep for him."

Afternoon turned to twilight at Cressida Lock. The sky was clear with a low white moon already visible. A thin gray light, which offered no warmth, shone down on the marketplace. Mati padded toward the cherry trees near the exit to Sparrow's chamber. Reluctantly, he had agreed to join the Cressida Cats that evening.

Distracted by a fluttering leaf, Mati changed his course. The leaf caught the breeze and sailed a short distance with Mati in chase.

The cherry trees stood silently against the darkening sky, their branches fanning the air. Soon, the Cats of Cressida Lock would arrive, but for the moment there was only the small robin that hopped from branch to branch, twittering cheerfully. Crimson light expanded to the west. Shadows grew to the east. Against the robin's playful notes, a faint hum arose. High above the branches, amassing like a storm cloud, thousands of bluebottle flies drew together. They cast the cherry trees in darkness. The temperature plunged. The robin's song was drowned out by the humming, which swelled into a feverish, high-pitched whine. Suddenly thrown into night, the robin looked up. Its small brown eyes caught the swarm of flies above the tree. It watched motionless as the dark mass shifted. Its tiny heart went *rat-a-tat*. The glistening bodies of the flies drew into a heaving circle. The circle began to twist into dark shapes: a tall jagged spine, long limbs with dagger claws, a winding tail like a hangman's rope. From the hissing neck grew a sloping head with a narrow face, large pointed ears, and a mouth glittering with silvery fangs.

Far away in Zagazig, beyond a corridor lit by flames, under the archway of the rearing cobra, the Suzerain spoke: "I cast my sight into the darkness . . ."

At Cressida Lock, the monstrous cat hovered high above the marketplace, a cat formed entirely of flies. The creature turned its face toward the cherry trees. The flies screamed, clotting together to form black-rimmed eyes. And the eyes were searching. "I see him. I see the one, the sedicia; I see him!"

The robin's head twitched. *Rat-a-tat! Rat-a-tat!* went its heart. Its beak moved slightly, but no sound came. The grotesque cat stared down at the robin, its dark-rimmed eyes unblinking, drinking up light. With a faint shudder, the robin fell limp from the branch.

At the same moment, Mati swallowed a cry. He turned away from the fluttering leaf. Something was wrong.

Mati crossed toward the cherry trees. A fatal curiosity compelled him, seemed to propel his unwilling legs. He drew toward the cherry trees in spite of a rising sense of dread, despite a familiar voice that rose over the wind, begging him to stay away. He froze. A tiny figure was lying still on the ground and acrid waves were pulsing from it, catching the breath in Mati's throat. He approached, trembling, the fur on his back rising. A small brown eye stared at him, the beak parted, the wings folded. As he stood above the motionless robin, the specter that rose from its body threatened to overwhelm him. His heart quickened. He felt sick, dizzy.

The bird had died of fright. Mati silently absorbed the

fear still rising from its feathers, feeling his back legs fold beneath him. *Terror*. Terror surged from the limp body in waves. Mati shivered, looked up. He strained his eyes against shimmering storm clouds. Thunder roared from the east, and above him the air quivered, almost as if the thunder hovered up there, as if it were closing over him. . . .

A mew of horror jolted Mati back to earth. A short distance away stood the ferals. In a daze, Mati saw but scarcely recognized Sparrow, Pangur, Trillion, Sinestra . . . He looked from their astonished faces down to the body of the dead robin at his feet. A crack of lightning shook the ground beneath him. And finally, the rain came.

The
Second
Pillar

A Secret Alliance

The Suzerain was pleased—a rare event. Whispers carried the news around the court: the sedicia had been seen. True, he was far away—very far away—but Mithos had been on his trail for many nights and would find him soon enough. Mithos always found his prey.

"Things are starting to go as planned," the Suzerain told the Commander in Chief of the army of the Sa Mau.

The Commander bowed again, unsettled by the relentless chanting of the high priests. "Yes, O Great One. The old networks have not failed us. My spies have found a friend in our mission, far beyond the boundaries of your empire, whiskers away from the Tygrine's hiding place. A chieftain, young and hungry for power."

"I trust your people were delicate. You told him nothing of Mithos, of the mission to the south . . ."

"No, my lord. He knows that there is something precious to the Sa, something close by. We would have asked him to finish the job, but he is unknown to us, and I am keen to avoid any mistakes."

"*Mistakes*? There will be no mistakes!" The Suzerain's dark eyes bore down on his commander.

The Commander, who had survived many wars and had inflicted countless cold-blooded cruelties, trembled now. "Of course not, my lord. He knows no details of the Empire of Sa's interests. He rules a neighboring kin and has designs on the territory where the sedicia now hides. But he knows nothing of the sedicia. He thirsts for power. The promise of it was enough. . . ."

"Good. Keep it that way." The Suzerain was satisfied. "Mithos will take care of him, I have every confidence."

The Commander flinched. He had witnessed Mithos the Destroyer firsthand, and what he had seen raised the fur on the back of his neck.

"But I have a final trick," the Suzerain continued. "Just one more, in case . . ." *In case Mithos should fail*, was the implication of the Suzerain's words. "It came to me from the spirits. Remember, the Tygrine is still a child. And what does a child crave most of all?"

The Commander shifted uncomfortably. Questions like this made him nervous. "My lord?"

"You are a fool," hissed the Suzerain. With this, the Commander was dismissed. The Suzerain closed his eyes.

He thought of the Great Spirit Alia, his ally in the other realm. Alia had assured the Suzerain that the Tygrine was weak, that he would soon be destroyed as easily as a lion slays a mouse. And of course, the spirit had been right. Alia was always right.

A Storm at Cressida Lock

In an instant, the sky had blackened. The storm clouds had burst, streaking inky tears. The land was awash with water.

"Why have you done this?" demanded Pangur. His voice boomed over the downpour.

Mati trembled, shook his head slowly, lost for words. The force of the rain pinned him to the ground, drove him down. Above him, he thought he heard the cherry trees groan under the weight. He braced himself for further lightning, but it didn't come. He willed it to strike the ground beneath his feet, to split the cobbled marketplace so that the earth would swallow him up.

"You have brought great shame upon yourself," said Pangur. Then, to the nearby Cressida Cats, "All kin members are to convene at the abandoned warehouse as the moon rises to its highest point. There his fate will be decided." The great tom turned, the others following in stunned silence. Among them, Mati noticed Binjax exchange glances with his sister, Ria. Next to Ria, Domino stared slack-jawed, slowly shaking his head.

Mati blinked against the rain, imploring Domino with his eyes. *It wasn't me; it isn't how it looks.* He still felt short of breath, his legs splayed wide to steady himself, pressed against the earth by the force of the rising wind and driving rain.

Sparrow hung back, face downcast. He turned in the other direction, disappearing into the catacombs and the warmth of his chamber. Mati paused, then followed. "They will not forgive you," said Sparrow sadly. "Instinct can be impossible to resist, especially for a young cat, but they will not understand." He said this without looking at Mati, then took to shaking out his fur vigorously.

I have let him down, thought Mati. *He has taken a risk in allowing me to stay with him.* "I don't know how to explain what just happened." Mati felt shame rising from his sodden paws, even though he alone knew what had really happened. Or did he? After all, what *had* really happened?

"Instinct, my boy. You scarcely knew what you were doing. I know, I know. . . . I was young once."

"I didn't kill the bird, Mr. Sparrow." Mati's voice was thin. He thought of the thunder. Where had it come from on such a cloudless evening? There was something unnatural about the suddenness of the storm, something ominous about the bird's death. Mati's heart quivered in his chest.

"What you mean to say is that you did not mean to kill it. It makes no difference now. If I had found you, we might have . . . Or at least if it hadn't been the entire kin, perhaps . . ."

"But I didn't kill it. I found it. It was already dead."

Sparrow turned to look at Mati. His thick ginger fur hung in wet clumps, and water glistened at his eyes. He blinked, nodded, squinted with his weak eye.

"I heard something," Mati continued, "or at least I felt something, something not right. I rushed over to the cherry trees and found the robin dead. Mr. Sparrow, something strange is happening—I think the robin died of fright! What could have scared it so much?"

"You didn't do it?" said Sparrow. Mati could see this was all he cared about and all he had heard.

"No, no, I never touched it. It was dead when I found it. If you take a closer look at the robin, you'll see there are no teeth marks on it—not mine anyway."

"You didn't do it?" repeated Sparrow. His eyes widened with hope.

"No, I—"

"I knew it!" Sparrow sat heavily on his nest, ignoring the feathers that clung to his wet fur. Mati felt the ginger's immense relief. The sparkle returned to his eyes. "Of course you didn't do it, my boy; you wouldn't do it, not knowing all we believe, knowing what darkness it would bring. You wouldn't do it. . . ."

To me, thought Mati. *What he means is that I wouldn't do it to him.* "Of course I wouldn't," he agreed.

"It was just . . . just bad timing. We can explain that to the others." Although a large cat of uncertain years, Sparrow had an innocence about him that struck Mati.

"I don't think they'll believe us, sir. And I don't know that it was bad timing, not really."

"But you said you didn't do it, that you just found the bird by chance?" Uncertainty leaped in Sparrow's eyes.

"It's true I found the bird already dead, but . . . I don't know. . . . I just feel that maybe I was meant to find it; maybe I was even meant to be blamed. Mr. Sparrow, I felt something moments before I reached the cherry trees. I felt myself being dragged there even before I saw the bird, but . . . I also felt another impulse, that I should back off, even that I was in danger. It's so hard to explain. I think perhaps . . ." he trailed off. He was thinking about the voice that had warned him away. Had it been his mother calling out to him? For a moment, he remembered her parting words: "I will never be far from you. Look to the setting sun and you will find me."

Instinctively his eyes darted westward, but of course there was nothing to see in Sparrow's chamber. "I should have listened . . ." said Mati. He was thinking aloud.

"You know, Mati, you haven't been here long, but . . . I don't have many friends and . . . it's nice for me to . . . to have you around." Sparrow shifted uneasily.

Mati was moved. He wanted to make things better. He dragged his attention away from thoughts of his mother. "Mr. Sparrow, I will never be able to repay your kindness."

"Of course you will. You have plenty of time. Nothing's going to happen to you, boy, not once you explain. Don't fret. If you didn't do it. . . . Well, then it's not your fault. Pangur and the others will understand." Sparrow's voice was light, but Mati sensed his need for reassurance.

"I'll try my best to explain," said Mati. But he knew it wouldn't be easy. He sank down low to the floor, feeling the faint drumming of rain through the pads of his paws. He tried not to think about what the Cressida Cats would do to him. Fight him? Claw him to death, even? He shuddered. His mind wandered back to the strange sensations he had experienced before seeing the body of the dead robin, of knowing that something was wrong, of longing to find out what but being afraid to at the same time. He recalled the storm clouds that had hung above the cherry trees and the terrible fear that had risen in waves from the robin. His throat tightened. Had the others not felt it? Had he merely imagined it? Was he crazy?

No, the fear had been there, lingering like a ghost even after life had departed. Fear had stopped the robin's heart.

What could have scared the bird so much? What had the robin seen?

Mati washed his wet fur with fast, nervous strokes. Distantly, he heard the agitated river rising against the bank, a grim reminder that time rolled on, that soon he would be forced to confront the Cressida Cats. What could he do to make them believe him?

I should have realized that the bird was in danger when I saw it this afternoon, thought Mati. *Perhaps my senses have become dulled, or perhaps I didn't want to know. Maybe this is my fault after all, even if I didn't lay a claw on the robin. I should have protected the bird. I should have . . .*

Emotions muddled, Mati longed for his mother.

I know that I didn't kill the robin. . . . But I know that it didn't die naturally. Oh Amma, if I've done no wrong, why do I feel so guilty?

"Mr. Sparrow? Mr. Sparrow?"

"Humph!" Sparrow awoke with a start. "Is it time already?" he said. He had been dozing in the warmth of the chamber as Mati sat washing himself, lost in thought.

The rain continued to beat down on the marketplace, collecting in deep puddles. Shallow rivulets of rainwater ran into the puddles like rivers into the ocean, reminding Mati of the ship that had brought him to the dock. Not far away, the real river swelled, dark with sediment. The rising waters battered against the lock's metal doors.

Mati dodged the puddles on the way to the abandoned warehouse, Sparrow trailing behind him. Squinting against the downpour, Mati sought the moon. For a moment he spotted a thin white sliver dance above the cherry trees before it seemed to bleed into the black sky. He tried to gauge whether there were others already at the warehouse, whether their anger had lessened, but the rain distorted his senses.

They crept into the warehouse through a gap in a window where broken glass had long since been replaced by ill-fitting boards, Sparrow struggling to haul himself through. Everywhere there were cats. Mati was weak with panic. News traveled quickly here. Cats who had not collected under the cherry trees and rarely attended full-moon meetings had come to see the outsider receive his comeuppance. Unfamiliar faces scrutinized Mati: gray, tabby, Persian, Siamese—cats of every kind and color, including kittens only weeks old. Among them, Mati flinched to see Domino, who stood at a distance, close to the tabby siblings. Mati's eyes searched the audience for Jess, but he couldn't spot her.

The cats talked among themselves in spiteful whispers as they watched Mati jump down from the ledge. Shocked indignation had turned to rage.

"I'm sorry," whispered Mati to Sparrow.

"Not your fault, boy," said the ginger.

"Not his fault?" said Pangur, standing close behind them. Mati shrank; his heart leaped. *"Not his fault?"* repeated Pangur much louder. A hush fell over the assembly. "You have brought great darkness to our community. You knew of our customs and beliefs, and yet you chose to ignore them. You have killed the first robin of the harvest moon!"

Pangur's words were echoed by the assembled cats as if they were hearing the news for the first time. "He killed the first robin! Murderer! He killed the first robin!"

"I didn't—" began Mati.

"At least have the courage to own up to it!" cried a voice from the audience.

Sparrow was about to say something, but Mati stopped him with a shake of the head. "Please, sir, Mr. Pangur, I swear I didn't kill the bird; he was dead when I found him."

"See how he lies to protect himself!" howled Fink.

"Is there no end to his treachery?" added Sinestra.

"We saw him eyeing the bird earlier—it was obvious what he had in mind!" said Binjax.

A ripple of shocked caterwauls.

"He's lying!" said Mati.

"No, I'm not! And you told Domino you wanted to kill it—you said you wanted to go after it!" cried Binjax.

Mati turned to Domino in shock. Domino shook his head slowly. "But that was before I knew—" Mati started.

"He admits it!"

"I didn't say—"

"You told Domino!" Binjax could scarcely disguise his glee.

"I told him he shouldn't, and he understood," insisted

97

Domino. "He said he wouldn't. Mati," he cried in distress, "why did you do it?"

"I didn't do it!" replied Mati. "Please listen to me, if only for yourselves. I think there is something out there. I think it may have killed the robin. I think—"

"Murderer!"

"Coward!"

"Even now he blames others! He lies to save himself!"

"To kill a small, innocent bird! To disrespect our traditions and beliefs!"

Mati threw a desperate look at Pangur over the rising cries of the assembly. "Please, sir, it's the truth; something is out there, something dangerous. Please, your kin could be in trouble; you have to believe me!"

Pangur's eyes were dark. He addressed Mati in a low voice so that no one else could hear. "The only one in danger tonight is you, and no one but you is to blame for your predicament. I gave you a chance against the wishes of the community. I shall not make the same mistake twice. I will have you gone from my kin, never to return. And you would do well to heed this order quickly. The others will kill you if they get the chance. Already they are calling for your blood. I will not protect you."

Mati looked around him. To his horror, the assembled cats were rising, slowly creeping closer, low on their haunches, hissing, jeering. "He's a traitor! Tell him what we do to traitors here!"

Mati backed a few paces into Sparrow.

"Why won't they believe you?" asked Sparrow, despairing.

"Kill him, Pangur!" cried Fink. Sparrow shot Mati an urgent look.

Pangur spoke loudly, so that all could hear. "As chief of this kin, it is my duty to mete out justice. You have been caught committing the gruesome murder of our revered first robin. You have brought thunder and lightning to our homes. You have disrespected the memories of our founders, *Pirrup*: the Courageous Ladies Wilhelmina and Moullier, Consorts of Freedom. You have invited a storm upon your own head. . . . Leave the protection of the Cressida Cats immediately! You are not welcome here!"

"No!" yowled Sparrow, but his protest was drowned by whoops, hisses, and excited meows from the ferals.

For a moment, Mati's eyes met Domino's. Domino shook his head sadly and looked down. Binjax shifted nearer to the harlequin catling, reveling in the moment. Mati saw him whisper something in Domino's ear. Domino pulled away but he didn't look up again.

The assembled cats pressed nearer.

"You must go, Mati. The Territory is no longer safe for you," said Sparrow sorrowfully—then, suddenly, thinking aloud, "I will come with you!"

Mati thought of Sparrow's feathered chamber, of his denim lady and kippers, of his quiet, harmless existence. How could Mati let him forfeit this for a life outside the

Territory, a life that would take him from the only world he'd ever known to one of uncertainty and danger? "No, Mr. Sparrow," said Mati firmly, although it broke his heart. "I'll go alone. Thank you for all you've done for me, but it is time I made my own way."

"Are you sure, Mati?" said Sparrow.

"Yes, I'm sure," said Mati quietly. He couldn't meet the ginger's eye.

"Murderer!" spat Arabella, the beautiful Persian.

"A claw for a claw, that is what is said—a killer should be killed!" cried Fink.

"You must leave, Mati," urged Sparrow.

Mati nodded, turned, and sprang onto the window ledge. The Cressida Cats shoved past Sparrow to surround the ledge.

"Mati!" cried Jess, against the chorus of jeers. She had only just found out about the meeting and arrived late through the far end of the warehouse. Standing some distance behind the assembled ferals, she had not seen everything, but she'd heard enough.

"Murderer! Coward! Death to the coward!" cried the cats.

Consumed with shame, Mati scrambled through the narrow exit in the boarded window. Behind him, he heard their indignant caterwauls.

"Coward!"

"Murderer! Coward! Death to the coward!"

"Find the coward! Avenge the first robin!"

"Has it ever occurred to you that he might be telling the truth?" cried Jess.

The others ignored her. *"Murderer! Coward! Death to the coward!"*

"Binjax, go and make sure he doesn't sneak back to the catacombs," ordered Pangur. Binjax smirked and headed out into the stormy night.

"Hypocrites!" shouted Jess over the wails and caterwauls. "You kill birds every day without a second thought! Hypocrites!" She fought through the crowd of cats who pressed toward the windowsill. Breaking free, she leaped onto the ledge and tumbled out of the gap in the window.

Instantly, her coat was drenched. It was difficult to see through the downpour. Jess caught a glimpse of Binjax's silver tail disappearing into the darkness. She squinted, her eyes searching for her friend's russet fur. In the distance, she noticed a man wrapped in a raincoat; his black umbrella concealed his face. There were no other humans in sight.

Jess scanned the sodden marketplace. Mati was nowhere to be seen. "Mati! Mati!" she called. "Wait! I'll come with you!" Her words, choked by the ceaseless rain, were carried away into the night.

Heat at the Center of the Oak

Although scarcely aware of the cold, Mati shivered. Blinded by the rain, he lurched over the tarmac, ran into a puddle, backed up, stumbled, kept going. For an instant, the marketplace was illuminated by lightning. In that moment, everything was white: market stalls, the boarded-up church, the rising pools of rainwater. Tall iron gates to the nearby park rose before Mati like bony fingers. A wave of fear seized him. He hesitated. Had he not skirted around the park when he first arrived at the Territory? Had he not sensed its menace?

I am a coward, thought Mati bitterly. *I'm even scared of a deserted park.*

Black again.

Mati hurried toward the park. He shuddered at the thunder's fast reply to the lightning: close, very close. He slid under the iron railings and through a hedge, burrs and mud clinging to his flanks. He threw a glance over his shoulder. It didn't look as though anyone was following him but in this downpour it was hard to tell.

Maybe I deserve no better, running away like a thief, thought Mati. *I have lost all honor, and no cat will ever respect me. Even Domino thinks I'm guilty. I have let down Sparrow. And where was Jess? I suppose she never really liked me. But Domino . . . I thought we were friends. I should have known better—how could we be friends when he was still friends with Binjax, who's been against me from the moment he first met me? Didn't I see them together in the marketplace only this afternoon? How could I be so stupid?*

Mati made his way past benches and sodden flower beds, scarcely noticing his surroundings. Despite the rising wind and ceaseless rain, he ran onward. Finally he came to a gnarled oak, its ancient roots arching aboveground like writhing snakes, its branches stooped and knotted with age. A curious force drew Mati toward the tree until, squinting through the rain, he saw an opening at its base. He crept in, out of the rain, to find that the trunk of the oak was hollow.

"I have been waiting for you, Mati," murmured a voice over the howling wind.

Mati jumped. "Did somebody speak?" he whimpered into the darkness of the hollow oak.

"You carry much sadness, much doubt . . ."

Mati's jaw dropped in amazement. *The oak can talk! It knows my name!*

Lightning flashed through the gap at the base of the tree, and Mati saw a skinny white cat sitting upright at the center of the hollow oak. The space inside the tree seemed much bigger than he could possibly have imagined from the outside. The cat's third eyelids were drawn over each eye like white gauze, and her fur was thin. She looked older than any cat Mati had ever seen, more ghost than flesh and blood. Darkness enveloped him again, and he felt the shudder of thunder.

"I'm sorry; I hadn't realized anyone was here. . . . Please, who are you? How do you know my name?"

"There is much I know of you. We will come to that. My name is Etheleldra." Still the soft voice seemed to emerge from the heart of the hollow oak, although Mati knew it belonged to the elderly queen. "Step closer to me, Mati; come out of the cold."

Mati didn't understand why it should be much warmer farther into the hollow oak, but he did as she said. To his surprise, he found that toward the center of the tree, heat rose from the ground. Gratefully, he sat down in the warmth, waiting for this strange old cat to speak. In the heart of the ancient oak, the howl of the wind, the rain and the thunder seemed to still. For a few moments, silence fell.

"There is a great force at work in the lives of cats, a force not of this world. You have sensed this," said Etheleldra.

Mati saw her only in shadow. He feared her, with her blind white eyes, but he also felt strangely safe in her company.

She continued, "I shall know you better, Mati. You may speak freely."

"Thank you. It's only . . ."

"You have nothing to fear here. I sense the weight of the doubt you carry. You did not kill the bird."

"You know!" Mati was astonished.

"There is much I know, and also much I have yet to learn."

"You're a shalian. . . ." said Mati. Vaguely, he remembered being taught about the mystic cats who possessed gifts of wisdom and sensitivity. Who had taught him? His mother, perhaps.

"Long have I had only spirits with whom to speak," said Etheleldra. "This is the sacrifice we shalians make for knowledge. Between the territories I live: Pangur's Cressida Cats from whom you ran, and Hanratty's Kanks who dwell to the north of the park. And also between the realms, between wakefulness and sleep. The spirits keep me company, and they have been restless of late. I do not know why, but they have mentioned your name, Mati. I have been expecting you."

"I don't understand. Where are these spirits? And what are they? Are they gods? Jess says that hinds worship gods. . . . Are they ghosts?" asked Mati.

"They are perhaps a little like ghosts," said Etheleldra. "Certainly, they were alive once, before many turnings of the moon, and they are not alive in the mortal world any more. Long ago they existed like you and me; they breathed our air. And when their bodies departed, something of their natures endured."

"How do you talk to them? Are they here?" Mati glanced over his shoulder, peering nervously into the darkness.

"Not here, Mati. Not in the park. Not in this oak. Not exactly—I talk to them in their own world, a place called Fiåney."

A strange thing happened when the shalian said "Fiåney"—a hot pulse ran through Mati, a crackle of excitement that set his fur on end. "Where's that? Is it far from here?" he asked. His whiskers bristled. Suddenly, he had to know.

Etheleldra made a strange noise like a muffled sigh. "Fiåney is never far away," she said. "But you could not get there by walking, even if you walked to the ends of the earth. In Fiåney there is no grass, no streets, no sky above you. It never rains there, and the sun never shines."

"So what does it look like?" asked Mati.

"It does not *look* like anything. It has no borders, no colors—only the ones of your own imagination. Most cats scarcely know it is there, but Fiåney is always with them, and they visit it every night as they fall asleep."

"Is it the land of dreams?" asked Mati, confused. He remembered his dreams now and then. He sometimes wondered what they meant.

"Not exactly," said the shalian. "Fiåney is the dream-wake, the maze that weaves between dreams, that separates them and ties them together. It is the home of the spirits. You know of what I speak. You have heard it calling to you, throbbing through your paws, whispering in your ears. You were born with two paws in the dream-wake, two paws in the mortal world. Only the rarest of cats, those of outstanding abilities or learning, can enter Fiåney at a time of their choosing and stay there as guests of the spirits. These rare cats have access to a force of a kind you could hardly imagine. There is great power to be harnessed in Fiåney for those who are able to control it.

"But cats without your gifts are no strangers to the dream-wake. Even the least spiritual cat must regularly pass through Fiåney, although scarcely aware of it. As you close your eyes and sink from wakefulness, before dreams take you, you travel through Fiåney on the way to sleep. And as you awaken from slumber and struggle back from your dreams, you pass through Fiåney again. You may not know it, but on these brief journeys you brush shoulders with spirits. More than that, Mati, you brush shoulders with your second self."

"My second self?" Mati furrowed his brow.

"Did you never wonder how the light came to your eyes, what it is beyond your body that makes you who you are?"

"My second self?"

"Yes, your true self, really. You are young, Mati. You cannot understand it all now."

"But what's my *first* self?"

"Your first self is your body. The paws that carry you, the tail that balances you, the whiskers that guide you. A mortal cat who ventures into Fiåney must leave his body behind at the gateway to the realms. But the body must not be left for long. To travel too far into that mysterious land—to attempt to leap across seas, to cross continents—could spell doom. A cat could get lost in Fiåney, where only the ever-shifting borders of dreams mark the way. A cat might vanish in the spirit world and never find his way home."

Mati shuddered. "Why would anyone want to go to this place? It sounds dangerous."

"It is dangerous, Mati, more dangerous than you know." Etheleldra hesitated, as if deciding what to say. When she spoke again, Mati could scarcely hear her over the distant humming of rain and murmur of wind. "As I said, it is a source of great power for the cat who knows how to use it. Not all will use it for good. . . ." Her voice faltered.

Mati's ears flicked back. The heat from the oak throbbed against his paws. He shifted, blinking into the shadows. He had the uneasy feeling that others were listening to this conversation, though he could not imagine who.

"Be wary in Fiåney, but do not fear it," said Etheleldra. "There is much to be learned from the spirits, and it is from Fiåney that our feline instinct is drawn—instinct that has protected us through many long years in the hazardous world of the first self. From your first self you gain your five senses: touch, smell, taste, hearing, and sight. What they call the sixth sense—the feline gifts of instinct and insight—belongs to your second self."

Mati looked at the white-eyed shalian, wishing he understood. Suddenly he remembered the little robin and the scene at the abandoned warehouse. He shivered under his wet fur. "Maybe there's something wrong with my second self. I had a weird feeling before finding the robin, but it didn't stop me from going back to the cherry trees. . . ."

Etheleldra's voice was gentle. "Fiåney is in your blood—you should not remain a stranger to it. Let us explore the dream-wake together."

"Thanks all the same, but have you seen the weather? It's pouring," said Mati, feeling a wave of panic. Outside the oak, he would have to flee into a hostile night. He didn't want to leave the warm hollow, even though he knew he would have to eventually.

"I told you, Mati, Fiåney is not a place you reach by foot. You need to enter it through your mind. Remember what it is like to fall asleep? Remember how it feels moments before you sleep, as your mind drifts away from your body?"

Mati wasn't sure if he knew what she meant, but even as he pondered, he sensed a change in the air, almost as if the structure of the oak was shifting. The dim light in the hollow tree faded.

Finally, the shalian spoke:

Spirits, I call to you
Guide me, guide me
Into your solitude
Into the halls of memory . . .

Mati sat in silence. He waited, not knowing what to expect. His mind wandered to Domino, to the sour taste of surprise and betrayal, to the shame he felt at having let Sparrow down. Suddenly Mati became aware that Etheleldra's chanting had stopped. The warmth from the oak's base diminished. He sensed the shalian watching him with blind eyes.

"You must clear your mind of troubled thoughts. Release your senses. The spirits await you—you must be ready to greet them." She fell silent. Stillness took her again.

Mati realized he must do something but was not sure what. He tried to stop thinking about Domino and the others, to put his fears about the first robin aside. In a moment, he remembered the bird's staring brown eye, its feet twisted in death into tiny fists. He remembered Sparrow swiping unsuccessfully at a bluebottle, Jess's bright red collar . . . Mati sighed deeply, and as he breathed out he felt these thoughts melt from his mind. His breath slowed and his body became still, an inner stillness that spread through every hair and whisker. The heat at the heart of the oak grew stronger.

Sensing the change, Etheleldra resumed her chant:

Spirits, I call to you
Guide me, guide me
Into your solitude
Into the halls of memory
Where the age of Te Bubas is noble and long
Where the old live forever and their kin are strong
Guide me, guide me
Spirits, I call to you

Mati felt her words ripple through his body. His mind relaxed; his thoughts unraveled. He chased unfinished ideas, but they escaped him. Memory dissolved. He was entering Fiåney, the state between wakefulness and sleep. Mati was too dazed to be surprised at hearing an unknown voice in his head.

"You come here seeking guidance, Etheleldra of the Oak. And you bring a visitor."

"Yes, noble spirit, I bring Mati. You have spoken of him, and he has come."

"He is not ready to receive counsel," murmured the spirit.

"Please, Mr. Spirit, I am," said Mati. He had not meant to speak, but the words tumbled out.

"Not yet, Mati, you hold on to too much doubt. Etheleldra has spoken of it. First you must let go of the doubt. You must learn to trust your uncommon instincts, for

111

you have been endowed with them for a purpose. To ignore them is to mock that purpose. This is the first pillar."

"The first pillar!" exclaimed Mati. "You've heard about the pillars?" He sensed Etheleldra's white eyes upon him, although he saw nothing in the darkness.

"We embody the pillars. So little do you know," the spirit intoned.

"I don't understand."

"You will learn with time. There is not much more I can tell you now. Only that your father was a noble tom, and with nobility he fell."

"My father?" gasped Mati. "I don't remember . . ."

"A spirit-thinker, he died on your third day on this earth defending what he believed in. And a great warrior, like your amma. One day you may rise to be a fighter like her. The potential for both is within you."

"My amma? Please, please wise spirit, tell me more about my amma!"

"You remember her. And long were once our conversations in the halls of Fiåney. But her voice we have not heard of late."

Mati felt bitterness rise in his throat. "She's gone."

"Her voice has stilled, Mati, and you will have to cope without her."

"So I'm on my own."

"Not entirely. Something of her essence rises from the

west, as twilight falls. And close by, there are friends prepared to lay down their lives for you."

Mati gasped. "I don't have any friends, certainly none prepared to die for me. The few I had, I've lost."

"You underestimate them. Your judgment fails you. Judgment is the second pillar. There is also a third, but you will have to discover it for yourself. And remember, she who is lost must not remain so forever, for every day away from home brings her closer to the end."

Mati thought for a moment. The spirit could only mean Jess, he decided.

The spirit continued. "The one you doubt has loyalty that you cannot see. He believes in you. There is another. Do not judge him too harshly. He is young, and although his heart is good, his courage will fail him. Do not rely on him."

"Please, wise spirit, are you talking about Domino? I don't trust him, believe me! He told Binjax about the robin—he made it seem as though I killed it!"

"It is not safe—Great Spirit Alia approaches! She must not know that we have spoken. . . . I must be gone!" exclaimed the spirit.

"You can't go yet! Please tell me more," begged Mati.

"Not everything is as it seems. Trust your instincts; use your judgment. This will be put to the test. Soon. Very soon."

"Please, please, Mr. Spirit, I need to know more! Please

tell me more about my parents!" But even as Mati spoke, he felt the darkness lift and the heat from the oak lessen. The trance was broken, the gateway to Fiåney closed, the spirit gone. "I had so many questions," said Mati quietly.

"I know," said Etheleldra.

"Who was that spirit?"

"His name is Bayo."

"Will I speak to him again?"

"I cannot answer that. You are very young, Mati, and your future is yours to command."

"I should believe what he said, shouldn't I? I mean, he's a spirit!"

"Yes and no, Mati. Bayo is a spirit, and he is both wise and good. But do not believe him simply because he is a spirit. You will find great compassion within Fiåney, but there is also cruelty."

"What was he saying about another spirit? A great spirit? He said it wasn't safe. . . ."

The shalian shook her head slowly. When she spoke, she sounded impossibly old and tired. "Spirits were once cats like you—mortal creatures who lived in this land and slept under the same sky. Like you, they had a gift for communicating with Fiåney, and when their bodies died, their souls stayed in the dream-wake to wander eternally. Some have taken it upon themselves to protect our kind on their journeys between dreams. Others have sworn dark allegiances from the first great battle between the ancient cats, our earliest ancestors. I want you to be aware of that, should you roam around Fiåney alone. Remember what we have discussed. The dream-wake can be a dangerous place for a young cat."

"But Bayo is a *good* spirit, isn't he?" persisted Mati.

"Yes, Mati."

"He warned me not to trust Domino. . . ."

"Bayo warned you that he of good heart would nevertheless let you down. But do not judge too harshly. We are all of flesh and fur. Or we all were once."

"He said other things . . . that Jess should go home. At least I think that's what he meant. And things I didn't understand."

"You are better able than I to make sense of them, Mati. All I can add is that Bayo urged you to trust your instincts. And to use your judgment. You have a gift, and all gifts come with responsibilities."

"The spirit was right. I have been ignoring my instincts, and doubting myself."

"Of course he was right, Mati. It disquiets the spirits that such gifts should be neglected. This is your destiny."

"I'm a nobody. I don't even know where I came from. Nobodies don't have gifts, or destinies, do they?"

"And what marks a nobody from a somebody, Mati? Is it their blood? Is it the size of their territory, the power they wield? Did no one tell you that it is what is inside that counts? I mean what is *really* inside—the second self. Those most reluctant to accept power are the best placed to take it. And your instincts are special, however you care to describe them."

"I'm sorry. I suppose I just want to be like everyone else. But sometimes I do seem to sense things. . . ."

"And what do your instincts tell you now?"

"Now?" asked Mati.

Etheleldra did not reply, and they both fell silent.

Outside, Mati heard the incessant rain and the shrilling wind. Seated in the warmth of the oak, he felt nothing. He was about to tell the old shalian this when an unexpected sensation caught him off guard. Dread twisted in his gut. He let out a small mew. In a flash he felt turbulence, heard the swollen river groan against the bank, and saw the water charge like a tidal wave toward the catacombs. Heart racing, body tense, Mati gasped, "Flood at Cressida Lock!"

"You know what you must do," said Etheleldra.

"I must help!" cried Mati. He bounded out into the rain and back toward the catacombs.

The Sun on
His Whiskers

The rain smashed down as if it would never end. By the time Mati reached the catacombs, murky waves from the flooded lock were breaking over the bank and pouring into the tunnels.

What had Jess said about the catacombs? That they ran under much, perhaps all, of the marketplace. The market seemed deserted. But someone was down there; he felt sure of it. Where would he begin to look?

Mati remembered the words of the spirit Bayo. Instinct was the first pillar. He stood in the rain and tried to forget his worries, to let instinct carry him. Nothing happened. He felt panic rising in his throat. "Stop!" he ordered himself. "That's not the way."

Mati remembered how he had felt with Etheleldra as she had drawn him into the dream-wake. It was there, in Fiåney and nowhere else, that his instinct could roam freely. He sat between two rising puddles and closed his eyes. He wished he could think of an appropriate chant, but all he could think of was something he had heard Sparrow sing before mealtimes:

> *Mackerel, mackerel, smoked and sweet*
> *What a tasty little treat!*
> *All cats know it's perfect food*
> *Raw or smoked or grilled or stewed*

To Mati's amazement, he felt the air around him grow still. The ground beneath his paws grew warm; his whiskers tingled. His senses reached out along the maze of passages that stretched under the marketplace. His mind roamed around each abandoned chamber, some still warm with the imprint of their owners. With revulsion, he even discovered the long-disused passages inhabited exclusively by rats, now bolting from each available exit, their young held with startling tenderness between long yellow teeth.

Mati started to relax. There was no one there.

They must all still be at the meeting, he thought. He knew that Jess stayed away from the catacombs but still he made a special sweep for her. After all, he had not seen her in the abandoned warehouse.

Nothing.

But even as he drew himself back from Fiåney, Mati felt

118

something: the thump of hurried paws shuddering against tunnel walls—heavier than a kitten's, lighter than a grown cat's; the scent of a young tom, proud and ambitious. It was Binjax.

Mati ran to the entrance not far from the cherry trees. From there, he scrambled into the tunnel, water already splashing at his paws, rising at an alarming rate.

"You! I knew it!" hissed Binjax, stepping out of Sparrow's chamber, blocking Mati's exit. "I knew you'd crawl back here, even after the whole kin told you to get lost."

"I'm here because of you. You're in danger; we both are. . . . We need to get out of the catacombs."

"Well, isn't that funny! I'm here because of you! Pangur sent me to sort you out once and for all."

Mati felt earth from the damp ceiling crumble into his eyes. He blinked it away. There wasn't much time. "Fine," he said. "Let's go outside. We can talk about it there." He moved toward Binjax and the exit by the cherry trees.

Binjax took a step forward. "Talk?" he growled. "Who said I want to talk, *murderer*?" Suddenly he glanced behind him. The entrance by the cherry trees was collapsing.

"We have to get out of here, Binjax!" cried Mati. In the faint light, Mati thought he saw the tabby nod. "Where do we go? You know the catacombs better than I do."

"Go forward, right at the fork."

The two catlings scrambled down the tunnel, taking the right path, water lapping at their paws.

119

"Hurry, you idiot!" snapped Binjax, close behind Mati. "It's really flooded. . . . I've got to get out of here! Turn! Turn left! Again! Take the left tunnel!"

Mati was getting confused. "Are you sure?"

"You idiot, I said the *right* tunnel!"

After hitting several dead ends and backing up into the main passageway, Mati floundered in a rush of water. "Not this way!" he called back to Binjax. "I think this way leads straight to the river."

"Shut up, murderer! You think I don't know where I'm going? I'm a Cressida Cat; you're nobody. Go on!"

"But the water's getting deeper. . . ."

"Keep going, I said!" ordered Binjax, letting Mati lead the way.

The water swirling at Mati's flanks tugged him forward. Before he knew it, he was out of the tunnel and standing on the narrow ledge where he and the other catlings had landed to avoid the dog on Mati's first day at Cressida Lock. Water tumbled from the flooded tunnel, drawing Mati toward the river. He clutched the ledge and almost flew off it, hind legs dangling for a moment above the treacherous river before he dragged them up as the worst of the flood from the catacombs crashed past him. He hugged the ledge, panting with relief, fear shuddering through his body. *You're OK,* he thought. *You've done it—now pull yourself onto the bank.*

Mati heard a cry behind him and wheeled around to see Binjax spinning past him, over the ledge, down into the black water. Mati froze, peering over the ledge. Binjax was beating the water with furious paws. Mati watched him with horror. Silver ears sank below the surface. Binjax drew his head up, gasping wildly. Mati trembled on the ledge, ears pressed flat, tail at his flank. Then he leaped.

Scarcely aware of what he was doing, Mati fought the water to reach Binjax. The tabby was sinking, his head thrown back, his ears and eyes submerged.

"Hold on to me!" urged Mati.

Binjax didn't hesitate. He sank his teeth into Mati's back, tabby paws grasping his neck. Mati closed his eyes, gagging at the stench of the water. He focused on moving with the current and away from the hazardous lock, but a powerful undercurrent was drawing him back, dragging him down.

"Over here!" called Jess. She was standing high above the lock, along the bank, blinking through the rain. "Climb on that!"

Mati saw the remains of a discarded bicycle leaning against the bank. One wheel, the seat, and a mudguard poked above the water. He changed course with difficulty and strained toward it. He was flagging under Binjax's weight. *I'm not going to make it!* he thought desperately.

"You're so close, Mati. . . . Just a bit farther—come on!" shouted Jess. Distantly he heard her tinkling bell.

He couldn't see her anymore, couldn't look up. He paddled wildly. His head dropped for a moment and he swallowed mouthfuls of foul water. His eyes were burning. He hardly realized that he had reached the bicycle until he felt Binjax's grip loosen. The silver tabby scrambled over Mati's head and sprang onto the saddle, then up onto the bank.

"Mati!" Now Domino was calling him. He felt dizzy. Suddenly released from Binjax's weight, he was as light as a drifting leaf. "Jump onto the saddle!" Domino urged.

"I can't," Mati moaned.

"Jump onto the saddle! Come on, Mati, just jump onto the saddle!"

He reached up a paw and buried his unsheathed claws into the foam of the saddle. Now he was hooked on but too weak to leap up. The bicycle began to stir.

"It's going to fall, Mati. . . . You have to jump *now!*" cried Jess. He caught the frantic tinkling of her bell.

Unable to spring up, Mati painfully drew his body onto the saddle. It swayed in the water. Mati remembered the sun on his whiskers, the salty sweet smell of fresh sardines. With his remaining strength, he sprang off the saddle and onto the bank. The saddle collapsed, the bicycle disappearing completely under the black water. Mati fell gasping among the weeds.

Jess and Domino were standing over him. A few paces away stood Pangur and Trillion, staring in amazement.

"You're OK," said Jess quietly.

"I'm OK," echoed Mati. He didn't feel it, though. He felt exhausted, sickened by the filthy water that clung to his fur. "Where's Binjax?"

Jess frowned at him. "Gone."

"Gone?"

"He ran past me. I wasn't really watching at the time. He didn't even stop to make sure you were safe."

Mati closed his eyes, absorbing her words.

On the far bank of the river, against a rising moon, a figure watched in the long grass. His bright green eyes scanned Cressida Lock. His pink tongue flickered over his teeth. "By the spirits," whispered the figure. "His market paradise is drowning. It's just as the Sa said it would be. Will his kin follow him when their homes are destroyed by the flood and there's no food left?"

Pangur glanced up from the near bank. Someone was shifting in the grass beyond, just out of sight. For an instant, green eyes flashed at him. The Cressida chief stepped back from the edge of the bank. "Perhaps . . . ? But no, he wouldn't dare!"

"Who wouldn't dare?" asked Trillion.

Pangur tore his eyes away from the far bank. "Nobody. I just saw my shadow on the grass."

A Shadow
on the Grass

Ferals who had risked the flooded marketplace in search of prey soon returned to the comfort of the abandoned warehouse. The rain had stopped, but it would be days before the catacombs would be dry enough for the Cressida Cats to return to their homes. That night the kin slept in the warehouse, curled paw-to-tail in family groupings for warmth. Mati slept close to Sparrow and Jess; Domino rested against his mother, Trillion.

Only Chief Pangur was awake, pacing restlessly near his sleeping kin. His brilliant green eyes settled on Mati, who awoke immediately. "Come," whispered Pangur.

Mati followed him out of the warehouse and onto the stall from which the full-moon meetings were conducted. The first shimmer of dawn hung in the east. "You want me to leave," said Mati. Why, after all, should the flood have changed anything? They still believed him to be guilty of killing the first robin of the harvest moon, didn't they?

"No, Mati. I think I was wrong about you. You saved Binjax's life. That showed quick thinking and courage. I should have let you explain about the robin. Do you forgive me?"

Mati was surprised. "Yes."

"Good. Let me share something with you, Mati. I saw my dark side tonight, and it scared me. Sometimes, a cat can be governed by the wrong thing, a desire to please his kin. . . . It's not always easy to make the right decision. Perhaps you will be a leader one day, and you'll know what I mean."

Unlikely, thought Mati. *Who would follow me?*

"What happened to the robin?"

"I found it," said Mati. "I think it must have died only moments earlier. I think it died of fright. I don't know why. Something in the air was wrong, but I can't explain what. I don't know who killed it. I have a very bad feeling." All this poured from Mati's mouth quite freely. He stopped. It sounded ridiculous.

Nevertheless, Pangur nodded. "And this flood?"

"The flood? That's just the rain, isn't it? The river burst its banks."

"I'll admit I haven't seen many winters here. Those who have have never seen such a thing."

"But what else could it be, Mr. Pangur?" asked Mati.

"I don't know." Pangur shook his head. "I don't know,

but . . . I sense the hand of hinds. Does that sound foolish?" The chief turned his bright green eyes on Mati, and for the first time Mati realized how young he really was, how unsure of himself.

"It doesn't sound foolish. I was recently told to trust my instincts. Perhaps you should trust yours."

Immediately Mati feared that his advice would be considered insolent, but Pangur smiled. "You're pretty wise for a catling. Come, that's enough of such talk."

"And I . . ."

"Stay for now. Your senses are powerful. We will put them to good service."

"Thank you, Mr. Pangur." Mati returned exhausted to sprawl at Sparrow's side, leaving the troubled chief alone on the empty stall.

The next day, officers of the local town council were dotted about the vacant stalls, jotting things down in notebooks and talking among themselves. The Cressida Cats watched from a distance. No one commented on Mati's still being there, nor on Binjax's rescue the night before, although the news had spread fast. Binjax himself was nowhere to be seen.

Mati was standing near the warehouse with Jess. Sparrow had gone in search of his "denim lady" and breakfast.

"I wonder how soon the catacombs will be dry," said Jess.

"Even once they are, the water damage will make some unusable. A few of the tunnel walls were caving in."

Domino joined them. Mati felt uncomfortable. He was happy to see Domino, but his feelings were still muddled. Hadn't Domino accused him before the entire community of plotting to kill the first robin?

Two of the humans had come to stand a short distance away. Mati, who rarely paid attention to the warbling of men and women, suddenly pricked up his ears.

"Definitely left open . . ." said the first.

"Are you sure?"

"Absolutely. Whoever did it must have had a key."

"But why would anyone want to flood the lock?"

"Slow down! I'm not suggesting it was intentional."

"I thought you said—"

"I said someone opened the gates to the lock, but they probably meant to get through with their boat and just forgot to close the lock behind them."

"Pretty strange that they'd forget."

"I agree, but how else do you explain this mess?" The man pointed to the murky pools that blotched the marketplace. "It's going to take all day to clean up, which means loss of business, but no one seems to have seen anything, and I doubt we'll ever get to the bottom of it."

"Not many people could have access to a lock key."

"Plenty do. Anyone with a narrow boat in this area, the lock warden and his assistant, heaven knows who else."

"Are you thinking what I'm thinking?" said Jess. Mati nodded. Domino, who, unlike Mati and Jess, was unable to understand human speech, glanced at them in confusion.

Mati was remembering what Pangur had said about sensing "the hand of hinds." He thought about what the humans had said. Why *would* someone leave the lock open, if not by accident? What did they stand to gain? It wouldn't really harm any humans. Humans didn't actually live in the marketplace.

Suddenly Mati wanted to be alone with Jess, to talk through his thoughts. He glanced at Domino. *But can I trust him?* wondered Mati. He wanted to.

Mati was spared a decision. At that moment, Trillion arrived to call Domino to lunch.

Mati told Jess about Pangur's suspicions and how they matched what the humans had said.

"Someone did this on purpose, didn't they?" asked Jess.

"Yes! No! Maybe—I don't know," Mati stammered.

Jess looked distracted.

"What is it?" said Mati.

"I've just remembered something I saw during the flood. I suppose I hardly noticed at the time; it didn't seem important. After you'd left the warehouse, I looked for you in the rain."

"You were there?"

"I arrived at the meeting late," said Jess.

Mati shifted from paw to paw. He felt ashamed that Jess should have witnessed his exile.

"I didn't see you," Jess went on. "But there was a man walking alone, a tall man. I couldn't see his face, and at the time it didn't seem odd that he should be walking around the marketplace in the middle of the night and in the middle of the rain. But it does now. Hinds hate rain nearly as much as we do."

Mati nodded. "Should we tell Pangur?"

"I think so. You waited for Domino to leave, didn't you?"

Mati felt a pang of guilt. "I'm not sure about him, after he told the others about the robin and made it sound as if I was out to get it."

"Maybe they twisted his words. I've never been keen on Domino and the other catlings; I've made no secret of that. But last night changed things a bit. He really wanted to help. I think he's different from the others. Perhaps you should give him a chance . . ."

Sparrow padded toward them, ears flat and tail low. "No market today because of the flood. No market, no denim stall; no denim, no denim lady; no denim lady, no breakfast," he said, with untold sadness.

Once Mati and Jess had told Pangur about the humans' conversation, things moved quickly. The Cressida Cats were divided into groups of five or six to seek out the person who had flooded the lock.

"But they'll be long gone by now," whined Fink. "Those

hinds on the boats pass through on their travels down the river. They don't hang around."

"Whoever did it is near. I feel it." Pangur's eyes met Mati's for a moment.

Mati nodded; he felt the same. The cats divided into their allotted teams.

Mati was in a group with Sparrow, Jess, Domino, and Trillion. It was clear that Trillion was still suspicious of Mati and Jess, but seeing Mati rescue Binjax had softened her. "If it hadn't been for that meeting last night, we might all have drowned in our sleep!" said Trillion. "I suppose we have you to thank for that, too, Mati."

Mati shifted uncomfortably. Her comment wasn't meant as a compliment. *She still thinks I killed the robin, and so do the others*, he thought sadly.

"It's the fishmonger. I'm sure of it. He hates us! Remember when he threw water at me, Binjax, and Ria?" said Domino.

"But we're looking for someone who lives on one of those narrow boats downstream and has a lock key," said Trillion. "The fishmonger lives in the end terrace just beyond the marketplace. Try to think before you speak, Domino."

Sparrow sighed deeply. "An impossible mystery, the workings of the hind brain."

Mati and the others in his team had made little progress before they were interrupted by a ginger kitten. "*Pirrup*: the

Courageous Chief Pangur, Lord of the Realm, requests the urgent presence of all members at the abandoned warehouse," said the kitten self-importantly.

Mati, Sparrow, Domino, Trillion, and Jess followed the other cats into the warehouse. Pangur stood in front of them with Binjax and Ria at his side.

"Cats of Cressida Lock," began Pangur. "You are all by now aware that last night's flood was no accident. The flooding of the catacombs was a direct attack on our way of life, caused by the opening of the lock. The flood has meant that the market is closed today, and that means no food. Much worse, it could easily have led to the death of our own, and almost did."

The cats turned to Binjax, who glared ahead, unblinking.

"Thanks to a team led by Sinestra and Kroof and their children, Binjax and Ria, we now know the identity of the responsible hind."

Whispers from the assembly. Mati glanced at Binjax, who met his eye for a second before looking away. He looked smug.

"As some of you already suspected," Pangur went on, "it was the fishmonger who opened the gates of the lock and flooded the catacombs. Binjax and Ria discovered through their grandamma that although the fishmonger does not own a narrow boat, he used to."

More whispers from the Cressida Cats, exchanged glances, cries of "I knew it!" and "That monster!"

"You see!" said Domino to his mother.

"Quiet!" snapped Pangur, and the assembled cats immediately hushed. "We think the fishmonger still has the key to the lock. As you know, he lives in the last house in the terrace bordering the marketplace, and we have been keeping him under watch. Does he think cats are stupid?"

A roar of curses and caterwauls from the Cressida Cats followed. But Mati was silent, his brow furrowed.

"Make no mistake, we will get rid of the fishmonger. Tonight! This is the plan. . . ."

That night, a team of twelve Cressida Cats, led by Pangur, broke into the fishmonger's house. Among them were Mati, Domino, Binjax, and Ria. Jess had not been invited. Both Binjax and Ria ignored Mati; not a word was uttered about the night before. The other ferals, although no longer openly hostile, kept their distance.

Pangur led the cats up the trunk of an apple tree, along a low branch, and through a small open window into the fishmonger's downstairs bathroom. They streamed in soundlessly, gathering in the dark hallway at the foot of the stairs.

Pangur stood on the first step and turned to Mati. "Where is he?"

"Third door," whispered Mati. "His breathing is slow and deep—he must be sleeping."

"Good," said Pangur. "Let us welcome his dreams."

That night, the fishmonger awoke to a chorus of meows and caterwauls. Green eyes flashed at him from his bed, from inside his wardrobe, from out of his sock drawer, and from his bedside table.

"Get away from me, vermin!" he screamed, eyes bulging. But he made no move to approach the cats. "You!" he cried, pointing an accusing finger at Pangur, who crouched at the foot of his bed.

Pangur hissed at the man, hairs on end. He drew closer, his black fur melting into the darkness. Only his bright green eyes were clearly visible.

The fishmonger's tone changed, became more friendly. "It was only a joke, a laugh; I didn't really mean to upset you cats. . . . I just thought a little flood might move you along to another place, would keep you away from my fish. I didn't mean it—there's space enough for all of us!"

Pangur took a step closer, a growl emerging from deep in his throat. In the surrounding darkness, the other cats spat and hissed. Then, just as quickly as they had arrived to invade the fishmonger's dreams, the cats had gone.

The next day the ferals saw no sign of the fishmonger, although the other market vendors had returned to business. The day after, a large wooden sign in front of his house announced that it was FOR SALE. A fruit-and-vegetable vendor replaced him at his stall.

❖   ❖   ❖

Several days after the fishmonger had hastily departed, Mati, Domino, and Jess were sharing their thoughts at the cherry trees.

"What I still don't understand is why you came back to the catacombs after you left Cressida Lock," said Jess.

"I met Etheleldra. . . . I haven't told you about that, have I? She told me to trust my instincts and—"

"Ethel *what?*" asked Domino.

"You know, the shalian, Etheleldra. She enters Fiåney; she can talk to spirits! She lives in the hollow oak in the park next to the river."

"I've never heard of her," said Domino doubtfully. He exchanged glances with Jess.

"I'm not making it up!" said Mati.

"We believe you; thousands wouldn't!" replied Domino playfully.

"It's true!"

"OK, calm down, fella! Why don't you show us?"

"Fine. Follow me," said Mati, slightly annoyed. He began to retrace his steps under the iron railings of the park and through the hedge, Jess and Domino close at his heels. He hesitated. On the night of the flood, it had been dark, and difficult to see because of the rain. It took him a moment to get his bearings.

The catlings pressed on, past park benches where groups of humans drank from a shared bottle.

"But I don't understand," said Mati, puzzled. "The oak was here."

"Here? Are you *sure?*" asked Domino.

"I thought it was, but . . ." Mati looked around. Everything seemed different somehow.

"Are we lost?" said Domino. "We don't want to be lost in this park. Amma doesn't like me going here. Some say it's haunted!"

"Lost?" Jess seemed faintly amused.

"We're lost, aren't we, if we don't know where we are?" replied Domino.

Mati pondered this for a moment. "But I haven't known where I am for a long time."

"Then perhaps you're lost like me?" said Jess. "You know you have a home, but you don't know how to get there."

"Yes," agreed Mati. "I do have a home somewhere . . . or at least, I used to."

"But that's a different kind of lost." Jess sat and began to wash her face.

"Different how?" asked Domino.

"Well, we know how to get to the marketplace. We'll make our way back to the cherry trees. Perhaps Mati will meet Sparrow, perhaps you will find a meal, and I will go back to the locked old stall overgrown with weeds, the one at the far end of the marketplace. We won't be lost then, not in the way we are now. But I at least will still be lost, lost in the real sense, because although I will know where I am, it won't be my home."

"But you could make it your home, couldn't you?" said Domino.

"I have only one true home."

"But you have a shelter at the marketplace."

"Home is more than a shelter. More than food, water, or comfort."

"What is it, then?" asked Mati. He and Domino pricked up their ears.

"Home is . . . a feeling."

Mati was intrigued. He opened his mouth to speak, but Jess had already turned toward the marketplace, leaving him with Domino.

"Poor Jess," said Domino, as if realizing her plight for the first time.

Mati looked about again, pawing the ground as if the hollow oak might emerge from it. *Where is my home?* he wondered. *The shalian, Etheleldra, knew things about me, and now I can't find her. I'll probably never enter Fiåney again, I'll never know who I am, and I'll always be lost, just like Jess.*

Mati was almost envious of Jess and her missing human. *At least she knows who to grieve for,* he said to himself. Suddenly he thought of the dead robin, lying underneath the cherry trees. A warm wind flattened his fur against his face. *Soon, Mati,* it seemed to whisper.

Where the Heart Is

"**W**hat's wrong, Mati?" asked Jess. They were sitting under the cherry trees, watching people buzz about the marketplace. The death of the first robin of the harvest moon had marked the start of winter. The temperature had dropped at Cressida Lock; the trees were bare. It had not rained since the night of the flood, and gradually life on the marketplace was returning to normal. Most of the cats had moved back to their chambers in the catacombs, Sparrow and Mati included.

"Binjax," sighed Mati.

"Just forget him. He's nasty and ungrateful. You can't expect anything better from him."

"That's not what I meant. Don't you think it all seems so easy?"

"What seems easy?"

"I mean, Binjax and his family discover it's the fishmonger who flooded the lock, the one person everyone suspected, and we get rid of the fishmonger, and that's that?"

"Why not?" asked Jess. "Anyway, you said the fishmonger as good as confessed."

"He did, but . . . Why was Binjax in the catacombs that night? I think he was up to something. I have a feeling this whole thing also involved a cat, not just the fishmonger."

"Even so, what makes you think it was Binjax, other than the fact you don't like him? It could have been anyone. You won't be able to prove anything. Just leave it—stay out of trouble if you can!"

Mati nodded, but he knew that he couldn't just leave it. A feral had had something to do with the flood, Mati felt sure of it. It was bound to have been Binjax. How, or why, he couldn't imagine.

Later that afternoon, Mati was sitting under a stall, thinking about going to Sparrow's chamber, where he was due for another lesson in feral etiquette. He noticed an elderly man walking from stall to stall with a younger woman and a little girl, handing out pieces of paper.

"Keep this, just in case; it's got my number on it," said the old man.

"Will do," said a stallholder.

And to the next stall, where a redheaded woman was

dusting off wooden ornaments. "Excuse me, I wonder if you've seen this cat?" asked the old man.

The redheaded woman paused to look at the leaflet and shook her head. "Sorry. There are cats around here sometimes, but I've not seen that one."

"Well, could you keep this, just in case? It's got my number on it."

Mati glanced toward the distant riverbank. He was considering Binjax and the flood. *I'm certain that a feral had something to do with it, whatever Jess says,* he thought. *And I don't trust that Binjax one little bit!*

The elderly man with the papers shuffled past the stall where Mati was sitting. One of the leaflets fluttered to the ground, and Mati saw that there was a picture of a cat's face with some black squiggles underneath. It distracted him from his thoughts. Although the photograph was black and white, and the cat in it a little plumper, he immediately recognized the large slanted eyes.

But why would they have a picture of Jess? he wondered.

Looking at the humans more carefully, Mati realized that the old man must be the one owned by Jess. The man was stooped, his winter coat ill fitting and his hair unruly, with a large bald patch at the back. The woman was probably his daughter, the girl his granddaughter.

Mati backed into the shadows beneath the stall. He didn't want the humans to see him, somehow to realize that

Jess was nearby. He watched them move away with their leaflets. A teenager trudged over the image of Jess on the ground, leaving the imprint of his large boot. This upset Mati, although he knew it was only a picture.

The little girl, the granddaughter, turned for a moment. She squinted under the stall.

She's seen me! thought Mati.

The girl was now approaching his hiding place. His first instinct was to run. Instinct, he recalled, was the first pillar. Then he remembered that judgment was the second pillar, and this made him hesitate.

None of the stallholders seemed to recognize Jess's photograph. Mati knew his friend's nature: she didn't go begging for food in the market square the way he and the ferals did. *That's why she's so thin,* he realized.

Jess's old man would soon leave the marketplace to look for her elsewhere. Most probably he would never find her. Mati suddenly remembered the words of the spirit Bayo: "She who is lost must not remain so forever, for every day away from home brings her closer to the end."

Mati wavered.

"Here, pussycat, here . . ." said the girl. She was slowly approaching the stall, hands outstretched.

Mati stepped forward, as if to let her touch him, only to back away several paces along the cobbled marketplace. He paused, watching her. She was a short distance from the deserted side of the marketplace and the locked stall that

Jess had claimed as her own. A nudge in the right direction would lead her to Jess.

"Aren't you a pretty cat?" said the girl. Again, she started to approach him. Again, her fingers had almost touched the tips of his large ears before Mati pulled away, walked several paces toward the deserted side of the marketplace, and turned back to her.

He glanced at Jess's stall. *The spirit Bayo told me . . . But I don't want Jess to go home,* thought Mati. *And she's happy here, isn't she?* He had made up his mind. Slinking alongside the girl he drew her toward the milling shoppers. Away from the locked stall—away from Jess. *Follow me!* he silently commanded her.

"Silly cat, don't be scared. Won't you let me stroke you? I'm your friend!" said the girl, walking and talking slowly, following him toward the center of the marketplace. This time he let her fingers lightly brush his russet forehead before darting away again.

"Hannah! Hannah!" her mother was calling her, glancing around the marketplace. "Oh, perfect! Now we've lost my daughter, too!"

"I feel tired," said the old man. "I need to sit down a minute—you get Hannah." He ambled toward a nearby bench.

"Are you all right, Dad?"

"I'll be fine in a minute. Just a bit sad, I suppose. I do miss my Jess."

"I know, Dad, I don't wonder—you had more meaningful conversations with that cat than you do with your own family. But we've looked everywhere. I think it's time we faced the facts—it's not coming back."

"She's not an it!" insisted the old man.

"Fine—sorry. She's not coming back. It's cold; let's go home for a nice cup of tea."

"Just a few more minutes . . ."

"Dad," said the old man's daughter, this time more sternly. "Jess isn't coming back. She's not the only cat in the world. We'll go to the animal shelter and get another one."

Follow me, Mati was silently instructing the girl. She kept stepping closer to him, almost able to stroke him properly, and he kept pulling away at the last moment, drawing her deeper into the bustling marketplace, away from Jess. As he did this, a strange feeling arose in him, a breathlessness, a throbbing from the pads of his paws. He silently reassured himself. *It's wrong for a cat to own a hind,* he thought. *It's wrong to wear the collar. . . . That's what all the ferals say. A cat who owns is never free. . . . Jess will get used to life here. She doesn't need that old hind— he won't make her happy.*

"I'd better go, silly cat; Mummy will be worried," said the girl, losing interest. She looked up, blinking through the crowds toward the deserted stalls.

Mati suddenly ran toward her, rubbing around her ankles. *No, don't look in that direction!* he willed.

The girl bent down and stroked him with delight, pushing

142

his fur the wrong way. He purred his encouragement, but he felt deceitful and his tail refused to rise. The spirit Bayo had said . . . Well, even spirits were wrong sometimes. Isn't that what the shalian had told him?

There was a small meow some tail lengths away, the tinkling of a bell. Mati froze, ears flat against his head, a surge of dread in his chest. The girl's hand was suddenly limp across his back.

"Is that . . . ? Jess! I don't believe it!" she gasped. In an instant Mati was forgotten as the child ran excitedly to the small tortoiseshell-and-white cat.

"Wait till I find her!" snapped the old man's daughter, peering left and right in search of Hannah.

The man was quiet, looking out sadly toward the crowds of lively shoppers. Suddenly he gripped his daughter's sleeve and rose slowly from the bench.

Squeezing between shoppers, stumbling slightly, was his granddaughter, Hannah. And grasped awkwardly in her arms was Jess.

Tears welled up in the old man's eyes. "Jess! My Jess!" he cried. "You are a wonderful, truly remarkable girl, Hannah!"

"I was playing with a little red cat, Granddad, and Jess just appeared!" She passed the small tortoiseshell-and-white bundle to the old man, who grasped her gently. Mati followed at a distance, slinking between stalls, tail drooping.

"Dear Jess! I thought I'd lost you forever, my little Jess-cat. How thin you are! Poor little thing! Poor little Jess! When we get you home it'll be nothing but chicken, chicken, and fresh tuna for my favorite girl! And Countess Catfood, the one you prefer—none of that cheap muck for you!" Jess rubbed her face against his, purring quietly.

Mati watched in silence. The humans were leaving the marketplace, taking Jess with them, as he had known they would. Mati was aware of a dull ache in his stomach like hunger, a dryness in his mouth like thirst.

For a moment, Jess raised her head over the old man's shoulder. Her eyes scanned the crowds until she spotted her friend. "Good-bye, Mati, good-bye," she purred, blinking those huge green eyes.

Mati blinked back and tried to look happy as Jess was carried out of his life. He watched until she was less than a dot amid the crowds and her tinkling bell no more than a memory.

A familiar face

The bitter days of winter crept on. Nobody mentioned the first robin of the harvest moon or the night of the flood anymore. But nobody befriended Mati either. A few of the ferals, such as Arabella and Fink, treated him with open disdain. Mostly, he was just ignored. Although used to solitude, Mati regularly wondered whether he would do better to leave Cressida Lock in search of a friendlier community. He stayed because of Sparrow, who had grown attached to him.

Mati missed Jess a great deal. Other than Sparrow, who slept all day and much of the night, his only friend was Domino. The harlequin catling had stopped spending time with the tabbies, claiming that they had grown "boring." Mati knew this had more to do with the tabbies' attitude to Mati than Domino was letting on.

Mati felt sure that Binjax had played some role in the flood at Cressida Lock. But as this was impossible to prove, he'd let the matter rest. He never shared these thoughts with Domino. He wanted to trust Domino, but he still felt uncertain.

The words of the spirit Bayo returned to Mati. "Although his heart is good, his courage will fail him. Do not rely on him."

One afternoon after his hunting lesson with Trillion, Domino came calling for Mati. The two catlings stepped out into the frosty air. The sky was a moist, leaden white.

"Amma thinks I should try to hunt more and eat less of what the hinds leave on the marketplace. She says I'm lazy." Domino was annoyed. "She keeps saying, 'Do this, do that!' But it's not as if I don't try! I'm just not a natural hunter like her and the rest of my family."

"There's more to life than hunting," soothed Mati. He wasn't sure what, but since he wasn't much of a hunter himself, it suited him to say so.

"Yeah, I know. But she's forever telling me, 'You've got to be a good hunter, Domino, if you want to rise to the alphas,' and I told her I don't—I don't ever want to be the alpha tom. She didn't like to hear that, I can tell you! There've been alphas in my family since the plague, she says. And I said there've been fleas in it since always! I mean, just because something's old doesn't mean it's good! And like I told that gray tom, I don't want that sort of power—not everyone does, you know!"

Domino was getting more and more worked up, scratching his forepaws against one of the cherry trees.

"What gray tom?" asked Mati.

"Oh, this was ages ago, before the flood and everything. Just some tomcat. Not a Cressida. Quite friendly—nice fella really. Asked lots of questions, though . . ."

"What sort of questions?"

"You know, what it's like to live here. He asked whether cats here are appreciated, whatever that means. I don't know. . . . Like I said, it was a while back; I'm a bit hazy."

"Try to remember what else he said." There was a hard edge to Mati's voice.

Domino abandoned his scratching and turned to Mati. "Honest, I don't know. I think he asked about the Territory— yeah, that's right, and the lock and the catacombs. He was really interested in the catacombs. And general stuff about life at Cressida Lock, you know, is it good and that."

"And what did you tell him?"

"I said yeah, it's great here; this is the best place on earth! I mean, look at it, we've got the market, the catacombs, everything!" Domino glanced over the marketplace proudly. "Reckon he fancied his chances at joining the Cressida Cats, because he asked about the drawbacks. Were there any difficulties, living so close to the hinds and that? Nah, I told him, only that nasty old fishmonger; the rest are OK."

"And what did he say when you said that?"

"Not much—lost interest. Wandered off. Come to think

of it, I've not seen him about since. Shame, really; he was a friendly fella, like I said. Actually, I tell a lie—a day or two later I saw him talking to Pangur over near the park."

"What were they talking about?"

"Don't know; wasn't close enough to hear. Reckon the gray was asking if he could join, because I'd told him what a great place this is. I guess Pangur told him no, they don't like outsiders here very much. Oh, sorry!" Domino fell silent, sensing, perhaps, he'd said too much.

Mati watched him, his brow furrowed. "Don't you see? He wasn't being friendly. He was squeezing you for information!"

"Nah . . . What kind of information?" asked Domino.

"You said he asked about the lock and the catacombs, and whether there were any drawbacks. . . ."

"So? He was just being friendly. . . ." Domino spoke slowly. Suddenly he didn't seem so sure.

Mati watched him steadily.

Domino's tail twitched. The harlequin catling was thinking. "Oh, fella . . ." he sighed finally. "Fella, I told him lots. . . . I told him about the fishmonger!"

"And you saw him talking to Pangur a day or two later?" Mati's mind was racing. He had been wrong to doubt Domino, who did not have a scheming bone in his body and found it difficult to recognize it in others. Binjax was a different case. Nothing could bring Mati to trust Binjax, but maybe, just maybe, the blame for the flood lay elsewhere.

"Yeah . . . Come to think of it, Pangur and the gray seemed

148

to know each other. . . ." Domino was concentrating hard, trying to remember, still one step behind Mati in his thoughts.

"He knew Pangur?" This triggered a memory. Quite recently, Mati recalled, someone else had known Pangur. Someone unexpected . . . "Oh, rats! Do you remember how the fishmonger reacted when he saw Pangur in his house? He seemed to know him."

Domino's eyes grew wide. "It's not possible! Pangur's a good leader; he's trustworthy—I'd stake my life on it!"

"Your *life?*" said Mati.

"The fishmonger pointed at Pangur. . . . He recognized him, didn't he?"

"It looked that way," Mati agreed.

"You understand hinds, don't you? What did the fishmonger say when he pointed at Pangur? Do you remember?"

Mati thought a moment. Suddenly, his ears flattened. "He said, 'You!' The fishmonger pointed at Pangur and said, 'You!' He *did* recognize him!" Other thoughts rushed into Mati's mind. "Pangur talked to me on the night of the flood. He mentioned something about the strains of leadership. I didn't realize it at the time, but perhaps he was sort of confessing. . . . He said he'd seen his dark side that night, and that it scared him."

"What does that mean?" The realization that Pangur might be dishonest distressed Domino a great deal.

"It means we can't trust him. It means we can't trust *anyone.*"

❖ ❖ ❖

"There you go, Countess Catfood. Only the best for my girl." The old man set down a bowl marked "Puss" on the kitchen floor.

Jess meowed happily, digging into her favorite treat.

"I've turned up the heat. Would you believe it's actually snowing? Snow in March! Who would have thought it?" said the old man.

Jess glanced out of the kitchen window at the gentle white flakes that tumbled from the sky.

"I've rather let my reading slip recently. I suppose I was waiting . . . waiting for you to come home. I never will understand how you made it so far west to the river." The old man smiled fondly at the small tortoiseshell-and-white.

She paused, blinked at him, and continued her meal.

"Now that you've been back a few weeks, I think I shall celebrate by retrieving my notes from the study. We can work together, like we used to."

When she had finished, Jess followed her elderly human to the study. She had not been in there since her return from Cressida Lock, as the door was usually kept shut. She loved this room best of all, with its musty smell of old books and curious ornaments. Immediately she found the warmest spot on a tattered rug by the radiator where she used to rest while the old man worked. Jess started to purr quietly, kneading the rug with her paws, glancing around the room. She froze. Her heart lurched; her fur sprang on

150

end. Up on the windowsill, next to a pile of papers, was a sculpture of a cat. And it looked exactly like Mati.

"If we can't trust anyone, who should we talk to about Pangur?" asked Domino.

"No one. Not yet," said Mati. They were watching the Cressida chief from a distance. He marched through the Territory proudly, black tail swishing, blood from a recent kill clinging to his muzzle.

A pale sun sank in a hazy sky. A faint moon rose. Dusk, Mati realized. A strange sort of time, between day and night—like the radiance between wakefulness and sleep. Like the shadow before dawn. Fiåney's time.

Suddenly, large white flakes began to fall onto the marketplace. Mati's eyes widened. He had never heard of such a thing. A wisp fell on his nose, ice-cold but light as a whisker. He turned to Domino. Distracted for a moment from Pangur, the catlings sprang after the wisps as if the sky were raining mice.

Slowly the cobbles took on a soft whiteness. Mati had never seen the marketplace so beautiful. "What's happening?"

"It's called snow!" laughed Domino. "It won't last long. It's very special!"

Mati nodded. He could see it was special. Everything seemed to be growing lighter, even as darkness fell.

As unexpected as the snow, Mati felt a hum rise from his

paws. He glanced at Domino, who had turned back to watch Pangur. The Cressida chief had almost reached the towering elm downstream, not far from the park where Mati had discovered Etheleldra's hollow oak.

Snow fell on Mati's whiskers and clung to his russet fur. He no longer noticed. A familiar voice was calling him.

"Mati . . ."

His heart drumming in his chest, he gasped in amazement.

"Mati . . ."

Hardly aware of what he was doing, Mati started walking in the direction of the voice.

"I'm coming, Amma. . . ."

He was crossing the snow-covered marketplace and heading upstream before Domino noticed.

"Hey, Mati, where are you going?"

Mati didn't answer. He trod between humans who were packing up their stalls and chatting excitedly about the snow.

Domino watched for a moment, puzzled, glancing back at Pangur, who was now sitting on the raised stall near the abandoned warehouse, looking out across the marketplace, a stark black figure against the snowy sky.

Mati was almost at the border of the Territory, far from the lock, far from the river with the weatherworn narrow boats.

"Come to me, Mati. . . ."

He hesitated. Something wasn't quite right. The voice . . . The voice wasn't quite right.

"Mati, where are you going?" repeated Domino.

Mati looked back at him. The hum from his paws lulled. He shook his head, narrowed his eyes. "I . . ."

It was starting again. The hum. Rising from the pads of his paws, through his legs, right to his black-tipped tail. Whiskers covered in snowflakes bristled. A strange warm wind pressed against his fur.

Mati started walking again, more quickly.

"You can't go any farther, Mati; it's the end of the Territory, it isn't safe. . . ."

Mati continued past the row of terrace houses, the last of which had been occupied, until recently, by the fishmonger. Snow was painting the world white, settling onto rooftops, fences, and trees. Still he kept going, his small pawprints littering the ground. Domino watched him and started following reluctantly.

Outside the invisible boundary of the Territory, Pangur's scent faded. The space around Mati shifted. Words became muddled in his head. He heard his mother's voice calling him. Or was she warning him away? It was almost as if she spoke with two tongues, and each was saying a different thing. She was very close now, he could feel her, very close but just out of reach.

Mati padded past bowing snowdrops that grew at the far end of the terrace, past twisted weeds nestling under new snow. He sprang up three high steps, onto a pavement he'd never seen before, pursued by Domino. Faintly, Mati heard his calls but they washed over him. The strange warm wind pressed against his back, driving him forward.

At the curb, Mati paused and Domino caught up with him. "Are you crazy? What on earth are you doing?" Cars roared by on the street ahead. The ground trembled under their power. Crisp white snow was already turning gray beneath their treads. Domino jumped back, fur on end. "Please, Mati, come away!"

But between the passing cars, Mati had noticed someone on the far side of the road. A cat, a beautiful russet-furred queen. Seeing her, he felt a tension in his chest, a weakness in his limbs.

Domino was begging him, mewling pitifully. "Why can't you hear me? Mati! Listen to me!"

Mati turned to him slowly. A look of happiness danced over his face. "It's my amma—I just saw her."

"That's impossible!" said Domino. "I thought . . ." He glanced out across the road, squinting through the snow. "Mati, there's no one there; it's a trick of the light. Come on, let's go home, *please.*"

"I *am* home." Before Domino could stop him, he was stepping out onto the road.

Domino cried out in anguish.

"Amma, I'm here!" said Mati. But something was wrong. Even as he looked at his mother, her features were changing, dissolving. He glanced to the west, where a red sky rose. Then, darkness.

The
Third
Pillar

One of a Kind

The hairs on Jess's back rose in sharp little tufts. She lifted a tortoiseshell-and-white paw in front of the sculpture of the cat, reached up to it, then backed away. It was as large as a real cat, tall and regal with a narrow face and huge pointed ears, a curved back and a winding tail. It seemed to be staring down at her from its vantage point on the windowsill.

"My dear, you look as though you've seen a ghost!" exclaimed her human, setting down his reading spectacles. The old man reached out and stroked Jess between the ears. "I assure you, it's nothing to be scared of, and anyway, you've seen her before. This is a sculpture of Bastet, the ancient Egyptian cat goddess. I've told you about the Egyptians, a remarkable civilization. It's thought the earliest domestic cats looked like Bastet—that beautiful long neck and stately gait. Well, everyone knows that. But here's something most people don't know . . ." The old man rose and shuffled toward the kitchen.

With a backward glance at the Bastet sculpture, Jess followed him.

"A story like this calls for a nice cup of tea. Darjeeling, I think. Hmm . . ." The old man rootled about the kitchen cabinets, where things were never quite where they should be. Coffee was stored in a tin box marked "Tea," and half a packet of cookies tumbled out of a jar marked "Sugar." The old man sniffed the cookies suspiciously, then replaced them in the "Sugar" jar.

Jess paced the kitchen impatiently, winding between his legs, allowing herself the occasional meow. She watched as he finally located a tea bag and filled the kettle.

"Snow didn't last long," muttered the old man absently, hunting for a clean mug. "Anyway, Jess, what I wanted to tell you is the Nubian story about the birth of Cat. Nubia is the ancient name for the area bordering southern Egypt and northern Sudan. Long before humans walked the earth, it is said that the first cat desperately wanted kittens, but she had no mate. Then she did something extraordinary, something that no cat has done since. . . ."

"Meow!"

"I'm just getting to that!" said the old man. Jess knew he liked to play this game, pretending to have a conversation with her. He stirred the sugar into his mug of tea: three lumps.

Jess watched, tail swishing.

"I'll tell you what that first cat did: she cried. Just two tears, one from each eye. And from those tears sprang kittens." He shuffled back to the study with his mug of tea, Jess at his heels, her bell tinkling. "It gets a bit blurry after that but according to the legend, two dynasties evolved from those kittens: the red-furred Abyssinia Tygrine and the spotted Sa Mau. It's said that the tribes wielded magical powers, a sort of feline sixth sense. The Sa were cats from the Nile Delta—that's in the very north of Egypt where the River Nile runs into the Mediterranean Sea. It's the same place that my sculpture of Bastet is from. But we humans have a habit of getting these things only half right."

"Meow! Meow!"

"I'll tell you exactly what I mean, Jess." The old man stroked her between the ears. "A lot of people know about the cats of Bubastis in the Nile Delta, but most have forgotten about the Tygrine. The Tygrine cats weren't from the Delta at all but from farther afield, as far south as Nubia, or maybe even northern Ethiopia. Ancient Nubian wall paintings show a cat with one side of her face spotted and the other side striped very faintly on the forehead. Nubia is the area now called southern Egypt and northern Sudan, you know. Did I already mention that? Perhaps I have a picture somewhere. . . ." He fingered the spines of several hardback books before drawing one off the shelf. "Hmm . . . Let me see. . . ." He squinted at the book and searched for his spectacles, finally finding them near the Bastet sculpture. "No. I can't see the picture. Perhaps it's in another volume. The one I took back to the library, maybe. . . . Anyway, it isn't important. The half-spotted, half-striped face is thought to symbolize the two kittens of the first cat. The Sa represented Cat's killer instinct, the Tygrine her insight and spirit." He sat at his desk, leafing slowly through the book.

Jess jumped onto his lap. He was often absentminded like this, starting on one topic and changing to another, and Jess didn't mind. But this was different. This seemed important. She meowed loudly, ears flattened.

"All right, girl, you want to know more about your distant relatives. It's natural." He scratched her forehead. "I can tell you something pretty strange. Some twenty years ago there was an expedition to find buried Nubian treasure on the border between Egypt and Sudan. Although the treasure was never found, the archaeologists dug up something else, something they weren't expecting. The remains of about ten thousand cats. Can you imagine that, Jess? Ten thousand cats, all in a small area—and dead for at least as many years! That's long before even the earliest stages of domestication by humans. Most scientists talk about full domestication of cats four thousand years ago, although it may have been as early as eight thousand years."

"Meow!"

"Do you see what this means, Jess? The ten thousand must have gotten there under their own steam. Very odd!"

"*Meeooow!*"

"I presume you're asking me whether the cats found on the dig were like the cats of today?"

In fact, Jess had been wondering how it was that Mati so resembled Bastet. She was remembering, too, her first day with Mati at Cressida Lock. He had sensed the presence of Domino, Binjax, and Ria at the fishmonger's stall, even before he had seen them. No ordinary talent, she had told him then. No ordinary talent, indeed.

The old man continued, "The answer is no. In very small ways, the cats differed from modern domestic cats. A little larger, slimmer bone structure—nothing dramatic. No one had ever encountered these animals before, and they must certainly be extinct now."

Jess stood up on the old man's lap and pirruped encouragingly, nudging his face with her nose when he fell silent. "*Purrrrr pirrup!*"

"Exactly what I thought. There's more to the story than meets the eye. Perhaps these cats were descendants of the two original feline tribes—the Sa and the Tygrine!"

"*Meeooow! Meeooow!*"

"The dig was canceled when the archaeologists failed to find the treasure and relations broke down between the Egyptians and Sudanese. Everyone tried to hush it up after that—I suppose it was a great embarrassment all around. We'll probably never know the truth. Some sort of huge feline gathering, perhaps? Or a disease that drove them to one place and sadly killed them off?"

Jess glanced at the windowpane. The face of the Egyptian cat goddess played upon the glass.

The old man sighed and dropped the book on ancient Egypt to the floor by his feet.

"A disease . . . ? No, not a disease. . . . It's so obvious! Why don't you see it?" This from Jess.

The old man ruffled the fur on her head. Her words, to him, were no more than playful meows.

She jumped off his lap and started to pace. "It's true!" she continued, knowing it was hopeless. "Two different tribes would never meet to talk. They would meet to fight! What the hinds have found are the ancient remains of a battle, a massive battle between two tribes. One tribe was trying to wipe out the other. Isn't it obvious?"

"*Meow, meow* yourself, Jess! I think I know what you're trying to tell me." Jess's eyes widened with excitement. The old man smiled knowingly. "You're telling me it's time for bed!"

The Fires of Sa

Several miles from Cressida Lock, a truck sped along a highway. It had been on the road since late afternoon. Pressed between boxes of computers, Mithos missed the snow, which melted almost as soon as it fell. In the darkness of the truck, he couldn't see the rising moon. But one thing he knew for sure—the sedicia was hurt, badly hurt. The accident had sent shock waves through Mithos's long limbs. He had known immediately.

Yet the child of the Tygrine Queen lived.

The truck rumbled as it skidded off the highway and onto a smaller road. It pulled into a parking lot in front of a warehouse on the outskirts of a city. Mithos heard the driver hop out onto tarmac and trudge toward the back of the vehicle. The back doors swung open, and the driver peered inside. Men from the warehouse joined him to unload the boxes.

"Come on, then, let's get cracking."

Mithos burst out of the doors and made a break across the parking lot, disappearing into the surrounding woods.

"Did you just see something run out of my truck?" asked the driver, slack-jawed. The men from the warehouse blinked. They had been up all night. "I thought I saw a fox or . . . I don't know. A large cat? But now I'm not sure that I saw anything at all!"

"You're imagining things," said one of the men. "Let's get these boxes inside."

In the palace in Zagazig, where the city of Bubastis once stood, the whole court had felt it: a shudder, like a small earthquake. The humans were oblivious. Traffic edged along the congested main road. In the bazaar, tourists haggled over souvenirs. Scraggy dogs sniffed for scraps on street corners. Pigeons perching in the treetops cooed cheerily. But the cats had felt it. And the Suzerain knew what it meant.

"It's coming together," he told the Commander in Chief of the army of the Sa Mau. The Commander shifted in the dreary chamber. "I told you, did I not? I told you what a child craves most? Not that you answered."

"Its amma, O Wise Master. A child craves its amma."

"That is correct, Commander. So I gave him his amma." The Suzerain laughed, a shrill, menacing sound.

The Commander studied the stone floor, waiting to receive instructions.

The Suzerain stopped laughing and his voice became serious. He spoke quietly, almost dreamily, as if talking to himself. The Commander strained to hear him over the chanting priests. "The time of servility draws to an end, and with it the darkest period of feline history. With the sedicia gone, my empire will expand across the earth. I will see our noble cause accepted by all and the old values restored. No more shall cats dare to live as parasites, dishonoring Te Bubas, mocking our ancestry, and spurning what it means to be a cat."

"Yes, O Wise Master," said the Commander.

The Suzerain turned to him, as if recalling his presence. "The sedicia is but a few breaths from death. I have made Mithos's job easier than ever. It hardly seems fair, does it?"

The Commander glanced up but avoided eye contact. "I am sure Mithos will handle the situation appropriately," he said carefully. "My lord, is there a particular duty I can perform for you?"

A bitter blue smoke spun lazily around the chamber. The high priests resumed their chanting:

> *Ha'atta, Ha'atta!*
> *Te Bubas, we call to you*
> *Your one true heir stands before you*
> *We do your bidding*
> *Lords on earth*
> *Spirits of the Sa are we*
> *Messengers of your legacy*

"Your job is simple. Prepare the fires," said the Suzerain matter-of-factly.

"But my lord—"

"*Prepare the fires!*" stormed the Suzerain. Several of the younger priests hesitated. The walls echoed with the master's fury. "By the full moon, the Tygrine heir will be dead." His voice was quiet again, scarcely audible over the chanting. "The Tygrine Queen hung on to power even as her empire collapsed. Those remaining Tygrines who were loyal to her cower under the protection of her remaining spells. I cannot touch them while her magic endures. But since the Queen's destruction, the spells survive only through the Queen's son, through the sedicia's second self, although he cannot know it. The sedicia's life protects them, but soon they will stand shivering alone without such sorcery. The fires of the Sa will burn. And so will they."

flower of the Desert

Over and over again, the sun wrestled the moon for dominance of the earth. Mati witnessed these clashes as violent battles, where the armies of daylight gathered to overthrow night. Yet the moon endured.

The vet hadn't minded the call after-hours, the visit at the clinic by an apologetic young man.

"He ran out in front of my car. . . . It was snowing. . . . I didn't see him . . ." He shivered on the doorstep, his coat in his arms. He lifted it so the vet should see the small, limp cat cradled among the folds of material. A beautiful cat with a ruddy golden coat, large pointed ears, and a long, winding tail. No collar around his neck. The cat seemed to sleep peacefully, but a small spot of blood on his nose warned the vet of his injuries.

The vet reached out to the little cat. "You're in luck. I'm not normally here at this time, but I got stuck on the way out, trying to settle some of our inpatients. About fifteen or twenty minutes ago, the three cats in the recovery cages started meowing like maniacs, totally out of the blue. I think the dogs were as surprised as I was. Almost as if the cats knew something the rest of us didn't! But that's crazy, isn't it?"

The man shrugged.

The clinic was built onto the side of the vet's house. For the first couple of days, she tended the little cat along with her other patients in the treatment room and left him to undisturbed slumber in the recovery cages. But it had saddened her that no one came to check on him. On the third day, the vet moved the young stray into her house and let him occupy a basket, feeding him with a drip. It was the same basket where, until recently, her old cat, Paws, had slept. She had lost him to kidney disease only that autumn. Often, she told friends, "There is a big furry hole in my life where Paws used to be."

Still the little cat slept. The vet had carried out X-rays. Remarkably, he had avoided serious injury to his fragile limbs. But he had received a blow to the head and was badly concussed. He had not awoken since the accident. Somehow, the vet could not face putting him down, even though she suspected it would be the kindest thing to do.

"I'll give him a few more days . . . just a few more days."

Mati knew nothing of this. Deep under folds of sleep, his

mind roamed. He looked out over expanses of darkness, shade upon shade of black as endless as the night sky.

"This is how it was in the beginning."

Mati heard these words without seeing their mistress. The voice of a queen, but not of his mother. A rich, powerful voice that seemed to draw itself from the immense darkness. Slowly, tiny specks of light emerged, salting the sky.

"The Creators drew light from the universe, as pure and hard as any diamond. They crushed it underfoot and scattered it onto a young earth as tiny grains of sand, forging a desert without beginning or end. It was hot and barren as the sun. Do you know what a sedicia is, Mati?"

The voice did not surprise him, but the question did. By addressing him, the voice had drawn him into this strange world. He had the sensation of being carried toward the burning desert. He was simply a presence without a body, just as the voice conveyed sound without a face. "No, I don't."

"A sedicia is a wildflower, a banished flower. Where no water seems to flow, under the darkness of rocks, almost without air, it grows. It stubbornly defies all the laws of the universe. It wills itself to be, and so it is. It lives even as it is hunted and destroyed. The miracle of life glows from every golden petal. It flowers for a moment and is gone."

Mati saw the scorched desert sand. He felt himself drawn beneath it, into darkness once more, where roots as thin as his whiskers sought to cling to the grainy earth. The tiny plant burst above the sand and a small bud formed, unfurling to reveal a single amber flower. Suddenly—in less than a blink of an eye—the land was alive with forests and oceans, mountains and valleys. Mati saw fish dive in the streams and rivers of the earth, antelope graze, birds of all colors and sizes dart between the trees. He was overwhelmed by the world's beauty. "Who are you?" he asked the voice.

"Can't you see me?"

Mati stared into the expanses of the earth, back to the desert where it had all begun. He had expected to see a giant, fit to command such a powerful voice. But there she was, a small russet-furred cat, hardly larger than any other cat, looking out over a riverbank. He noticed faint spots on her back and a strange white marking like an uncoiled serpent.

She turned slowly. She looked at Mati with golden eyes that tilted up at the corners between pointed, widely spaced ears. "Now do you know who I am?"

"I think so."

"Who am I?"

"You are . . . You are the very first of our kind."

"Yes. I am Te Bubas, the first cat. I was made by the Creators and the Creators are in my blood, born to be part mortal and part spirit." She blinked slowly.

In the moment that her eyes closed, darkness took the earth. Light returned as she looked on him. "And who are you?"

"I am Mati."

Te Bubas frowned. Her eyes dimmed. And soon the world was black once more.

An Apology

For the humans of Cressida Lock, it was business as usual. The marketplace bustled with activity, the human appetite for shopping endless. But among the ferals, a change had taken place. It started with the small earthquake that only they had felt, which had happened—it turned out—at the same instant that Mati was hit by a car.

A hush fell over the ferals. They had all sensed it, at the moment of the tremor—a strange sort of emptiness.

"Domino?" Trillion stood a few paces away in their chamber in the catacombs, watching her son. He was curled against the wall with his head resting on his front paws and his tail wrapped around his flank. He had sat like this for days, scarcely moving. "Come, Domino, come outside; breathe some fresh air. Eat something."

Domino shook his head slowly.

His mother continued, "You don't know what's happened to Mati. You said that a hind took him. They have all sorts of powerful medicines. I'm sure he's recovering happily as we speak. He's probably moved on to somewhere new."

"Somewhere where they're nice to him," said Domino flatly.

"Were we so bad?"

"Yes. Only Sparrow stuck up for him."

"I think Pangur quite liked him—" Trillion caught herself using the past tense. "*Likes* him."

Domino snorted.

"What do you mean by that?" she asked.

"You can't trust Pangur."

Trillion was shocked. "Pangur's our chief! You must never say that, no matter how upset you feel!" She glanced nervously toward the entrance to the chamber. "Anyway, Pangur is a strong leader. He has a good heart. That hasn't always been the case with Cressida chiefs; we should count ourselves lucky."

Domino looked up at his mother, wide-eyed. He hesitated.

"What is it, Domino? What aren't you telling me?"

"I can't! I promised . . . I promised Mati."

"Promised Mati what? Domino, he's not here, and we don't know that—"

"That he's ever coming back?" Domino looked down at the floor of the chamber.

This time his mother spoke more gently. "Domino, you have to have faith. I'm sorry if I didn't initially trust Mati.

It's difficult with outsiders. . . . He could have been anyone, and he didn't seem to know anything about himself. But I was there when he saved Binjax, remember? That took enormous courage. My opinion of Mati has changed. I suppose I think he's rather remarkable, although I feel a little embarrassed saying so."

"Really, Amma?"

"Of course. And Pangur has seen it, too—before I did, I'm sure. He mentioned something about Mati's instincts."

Domino's face changed, became closed. "Oh, really?" he said in a tight voice. "I wouldn't trust anything he says."

"Domino, why? If there's something wrong you must share it with me—I'm your amma!"

"But I promised Mati. . . ."

Trillion spoke with quiet authority. "We don't know that Mati's coming back anytime soon. That's the reality, as sad as it is. You'd better tell me what's been going on. . . ."

Trillion listened in silence as her son told her about Mati's suspicions that a cat had been involved in the flood. She frowned when he mentioned Mati's meeting with the shalian, Pangur's comments on the strains of leadership, and the fact that the fishmonger seemed to recognize the Cressida chief. Domino told her about his conversation with the gray cat, and that Pangur had talked to the gray a day or two later. He finished by mentioning Mati's odd behavior on the evening he stepped onto the road. "He said he saw his amma, but I swear there was no one there! He seemed so sure. He didn't listen to me—I tried to stop him! It was like his head was somewhere else. . . . It's really hard to explain!"

"Hush now, Domino, it wasn't your fault; you did everything you could," soothed his mother. "Mati is, I think, a sensitive sort of cat. Perhaps he can even talk to spirits."

"Do you think so?"

"Other than madness, I can't think of another explanation for his behavior. And I doubt that he's crazy. He mentioned a shalian?"

"Yeah, Ethel-something I think."

Trillion nodded. "Etheleldra. Mati saw her in the park, you say? Well, that's possible, I suppose. She lived on the market square once."

"Really? I've never heard of her."

"I have. My grandamma used to talk about her. I never met Etheleldra myself, of course."

"What do you mean, Amma?"

"I mean she lived here before many changes of the seasons. She must have died long ago. And yet . . ."

"Me, Jess, and Mati went to find her in her hollow oak, but she wasn't there—the tree wasn't there—*nothing*. But Mati swore she'd been there."

"Some things can't be explained. Perhaps she was there one day, gone the next. 'A cat of unparalleled wisdom,' my grandamma called her. Etheleldra would enter Fiåney and talk to spirits. A cat like that is very rare. Perhaps she has

174

become part spirit herself. Who knows?"

Domino shifted uncomfortably. "Don't you know?"

"No, child. There are some things even I don't know."

Domino frowned. "I don't get it. How come Mati could talk to Etheleldra, but me and Jess couldn't?"

"It's hard to say, Domino. Perhaps he has something of the shalian in his blood. After all, we know next to nothing of his parentage. His amma could be anyone. She could even have been a shalian herself!"

"Yeah, I suppose so," said Domino doubtfully.

"I feel it's somehow connected with what's going on here . . . whatever *is* going on here. But what worries me most right now is what you've told me about Pangur. I trusted Pangur. I can't believe he would seek to harm us."

"But the fishmonger recognized him! And Pangur knew the gray cat, and Mati said that cat wasn't being friendly but was squeezing me for information! How else do you explain it? And how about that weird thing Pangur said to Mati, about seeing his dark side?"

Trillion sat quietly for a moment. "Pangur said something a bit strange to me, too. I hardly thought of it at the time. It was the night of the flood, and Mati had just rescued Binjax. I was standing a short distance from the bank with Pangur. I caught him looking out over the water. He had a strange look on his face. He said he'd seen his shadow on the grass. But now that I think of it, that's nonsense. It was the middle of the night and raining heavily. There couldn't have been any shadows!"

Domino shook his head, bewildered.

"I'm going to talk to Pangur," said Trillion decisively.

"Amma, you can't! I promised Mati!"

"No, Domino! I'm going to confront him about this. You stay here!" She trotted out of the chamber and through the catacombs.

After only a moment's hesitation, Domino dashed after her, moving quickly for the first time in days.

They strode past Arabella and Fink, who sat under a stall on the cobbled marketplace.

"Is there something wrong?" asked Fink nosily.

"No!" snapped Trillion.

Arabella and Fink exchanged glances. In a moment, they were trailing behind Trillion and Domino. The cats passed Sinestra and her husband Kroof, who were busy schooling Binjax and Ria, and onward past Sparrow who sat, depressed, under the cherry trees. Soon, the ferals were following Trillion and her nervous son, whispering of a confrontation with Pangur.

They found him at his familiar stall, overlooking the marketplace. From this vantage point, Pangur looked out upon the market square with the boarded-up church, the riverbank, the lock. He frowned when he saw his approaching kin.

Trillion stopped before the stall, glaring up at Pangur with her jaw set. Domino sat by her side; the rest of the Cressida Cats stood a couple of paces behind them.

"What's going on?" demanded Pangur. His voice was calm, but his tail swished back and forth uneasily.

"I wanted to ask you the same question," returned Trillion defiantly. Domino stared at his mother with newfound respect.

Pangur listened in silence as Trillion repeated Domino's story. She left out any mention of the shalian and Mati's strange behavior before the accident. Instead she focused on the fishmonger and Domino's meeting with the gray cat. Pangur's face was grave.

"You told Mati that you saw your dark side and it scared you. You told me that you saw your shadow on the grass. And then there's the fishmonger. The fishmonger pointed at you!" With this, she fell silent.

The Cressida Cats had gasped and murmured during Trillion's speech. Now they hushed and braced themselves for their leader's reaction.

Pangur, who had listened steadily throughout with no hint of emotion, now turned to Domino. "You saw me talk to this gray cat? The cat who asked about the catacombs and the lock?"

Domino looked at the ground. "Yes, sir."

More gasps from the ferals, as if they were hearing this news for the first time.

"It wasn't me." Pangur directed this comment at Domino, turned pointedly to Trillion, then looked from one face to the next of his assembled kin.

"Sir, I'm sorry but . . . it was you!" blurted Domino.

"How closely did you see this cat? Were you standing next to him?"

"No, sir. He was over toward the park, and I was near the cherry trees. But it was you, I'm sure—black coat, green eyes . . ."

"It wasn't me, but in a way I have failed you all," said Pangur. The ferals glanced at one another, then back at Pangur. "I failed you because I suspected this but didn't act. I suppose I hoped that I was wrong. I should have known when the fishmonger pointed at me. . . . He did indeed point at me, and it surprised me. I should have known when I saw a cat watching on the far side of the bank on the night of the flood, a black cat with green eyes."

"You actually expect us to believe that you have some sort of double out there who's been up to mischief, that you are entirely innocent of blame?" demanded Sinestra. Angry meows rose from the ferals.

"I am not innocent of blame. I have already told you that I should've known. There are some we'd sooner avoid wars with, so we try to ignore the damage they cause. Mati was right. This black cat was undoubtedly trying to find ways to harm us. The gray was in on it, too, certainly from the same kin. They must have seen the fishmonger as a great opportunity—a cat hater who, with just enough baiting, was bound to take matters into his own hands. They can't have guessed what the fishmonger would do, but it was obvious he would attack the market cats. How could he have known that the black and gray weren't local?"

"As if you have a double! How ridiculous!" snapped Fink.

"I'm not talking about a double. I'm talking about my brother."

"Your *brother?*" said Trillion. "You've never mentioned a brother!"

"He doesn't have a brother!" scowled Arabella.

The others began to join in, gaining confidence.

"Why haven't we heard talk of this brother before?"

"Why didn't he come with you to Cressida Lock?"

"My brother didn't come with me to Cressida Lock because we're not friends; we're rivals," said Pangur. "He would have liked to claim leadership of the kin himself. He isn't far away, though, and never has been. My brother: my dark side, my shadow. I have mentioned my brother. But never by *that* name." Pangur turned toward Trillion, his old friend.

"Surely you can't mean . . ." she trailed off.

"Indeed I do. You will all know the name but perhaps not the face. We were both from the same litter, you know. I never thought it would come to this. Hanratty. My brother, Hanratty, who claimed leadership of the Kanks but won't rest until he rules the marketplace, too."

A wave of anger, fear, and relief ran through the ferals as they absorbed their chief's words. Pangur sighed, his glossy black fur shuddering for a moment, his tail jerking nervously. The kin was his again, but at what cost?

Brothers

"**W**e were born three summers ago, in a bunker at the bottom of a hind garden where they kept firewood. Three of us: me, Hanratty, and a black queen who didn't live to see her first sunrise or be blessed with a name. Hanratty and I were inseparable in the beginning. We would follow our amma around the neighboring gardens, scaring the house cats and generally feeling quite tough and proud of ourselves." Pangur's ears flicked back. He glanced around him at the kin.

They sat in silence, waiting for him to continue.

"I'm telling you this because I want you to understand it wasn't always like this. In the beginning we were friends, soul mates even, just as you'd expect from brothers. Our amma loved us both, would do anything for us, but it's true to say I was always her favorite. I was the stronger one, the bolder one. She used to say I'd be a great warrior one day, that I'd do her proud. And I promised her I would.

"When the time came to leave our amma and make our own way, Hanratty and I left together. I suppose I made most of the decisions, even early on. Hanratty was happy just to follow. That's what I thought, anyway.

"We traveled a lot in the early days, as young toms will. I took first pickings in most matters. It went without saying. Hanratty seemed content to step back where there was food, or pretty queens. He always got his share, of course . . . but not until I'd had mine. As far as I was concerned, I had earned the right. I was always the first to rise to a challenge by rival toms we met on our travels, always prepared to take risks. I never thought Hanratty much of a fighter. I guess I underestimated him in many ways."

The Cressida Cats listened closely. Nobody spoke.

Pangur continued. "I suppose that all this time, while as far as I was aware Hanratty was happy to let me lead, he was quietly fuming with rage, biding his time until he could get the better of me. Who knows when it started? Perhaps in the weeks when we left our amma and made our own way, perhaps earlier, when we played as kittens.

"We had traveled a long way from the wood bunker at the bottom of the garden. We'd passed many gardens by then, won and lost fights, escaped oolfs, and tracked the river from the dock. By the time we reached the park at the border of Cressida Lock, I felt it was time to stop, to build a home.

I told Hanratty that I meant to enter the marketplace and make it my own, that he would join me in a new order.

"To my astonishment, he said no, that the market kin would be his, that I would serve *him*. He said that he had been deliberately letting me lead all along, that it had been helpful having me around to fight his battles, that he had been waiting for the right moment to push me aside. I couldn't believe it at first. I couldn't understand how he had come to hate me so much. But I wouldn't allow a tom to speak to me in that way, to challenge me so openly, not even my own brother.

"We fought briefly. Hanratty was vicious, but I was stronger. I could have killed him, but I didn't have the heart. Or maybe I just lacked the nerve. Either way, I chased him from the marketplace. He ran mewling, promising never to return. But soon I learned that he had taken over the neighboring Kank kin and deposed their leader. I should have known then that he'd be trouble, that I wasn't rid of him.

"Long, bitter nights he must have called to the moon, cursing me, willing my downfall. And then on the night of the flood, when I thought I saw him on the far bank . . . But I hadn't wanted to believe it. After all, he was my brother."

The wind rose over the marketplace.

Pangur shook his head, as if shaking away a memory of kittenhood. "A strange little catling with big ears and golden eyes told me to trust my instincts," he went on. "But I didn't.

And now that catling has left the marketplace, and perhaps in a way we are all to blame for that."

The ferals shifted uncomfortably. Sparrow gave a small yowl. They all knew he was referring to Mati. Only Binjax maintained a blank expression, standing away from his family toward the rear of the ferals.

Trillion spoke in a quiet voice, all trace of accusation gone. "What do you plan to do about Hanratty?"

Pangur looked at her directly. Fond memories had faded, replaced with anger and the sting of betrayal. His eyes hardened. "What I should have done a long time ago. I will fight him—to the death."

Between Two Worlds

"You are close, Mithos, closer than ever," called the Suzerain through the swirling bitter mist in his chamber. "The spirits have spoken of a hind building, of cats in cages, of injured oolfs, limping and diseased. A house of sickness, where different kinds are pressed together. This is where you will find the sedicia."

Mithos crouched under a bush on the side of a street. He looked out over a bustling city through narrowed yellow eyes. His surroundings were immediately both familiar and foreign. They were colder and greener than his homeland but just as scarred by the relentless building of humans: their roads, their traffic, their effortless pollution. He craned his neck, whiskers inching forward, opening his mouth to reveal pointed ivory fangs. His sandpaper tongue flickered snakelike, tasting the air. Yes, the child of the Tygrine

Queen was close. Mithos could almost feel the slow rising and falling of his chest, hear the deep breaths that betrayed sleep—asleep and helpless. But where?

Again, the Suzerain's voice spoke to Mithos from his distant chamber: "I will show you. There are two paths to the same end, one in the world of the flesh, and one in the world of spirits. Fiåney, the spirit world, is our domain. Use it to trap him. Even if the sedicia has the power in him to use Fiåney for his own ends, he cannot know it. What can a catling know of such things? He does not even know who he is. As long as he remains ignorant, the Empire of Sa is safe.

"Let Fiåney guide you. Already you balance on the path between the two worlds. The Tygrine cat is vulnerable in both."

"Yes, O Master," murmured Mithos. He retreated farther under the bush and shut his eyes. The mysteries of Fiåney were many. Wise cats knew that through the dream-wake it was possible to cross space and even time itself, but only for short stretches. Mithos remembered what the Suzerain had told him as he first set off on his mission:

"Beware of Fiåney, Mithos," he had said. "Use it wisely. Wait till you are close to the sedicia's first self before entering the dream-wake and hunting him down. Never stray too far from your first self on earth. You could get lost in Fiåney and never find your way out. . . . For the cat who knows how to control it, Fiåney can unlock power greater than any force on earth. Draw from Fiåney. Use your instinct. You will know when."

Mithos was now within a few miles of the sedicia—he had sensed it. The time for the dream-wake had finally come. Here, hidden beneath the bush, frozen in a trance, Mithos would leave his body. Although his second self in Fiåney would not be far away, this was still dangerous. Under the bush, Mithos would be vulnerable to passing dogs. At the onset of danger, he would probably awaken in time to escape or fight. *Probably.* But there was always a risk. It was a risk Mithos accepted without hesitation.

Just as vision blurs when the eyes stare without seeing, Mithos allowed his mind to blur by avoiding thought. As he sank into Fiåney, the sounds of nearby traffic faded and the chanting of the high priests from the Suzerain's distant chamber encircled him:

> *Ha'atta, Ha'atta!*
> *Te Bubas, we call to you*
> *Your one true heir stands before you . . .*

Trees, buildings, buses, people: all distractions, all obstacles to Mithos spying the sedicia. He watched as they faded away. For a moment he felt an intense heat rising from his paws until all physical sensation disappeared. Now Mithos saw the house of sickness that his master had spoken of, where diseased and injured animals were locked up.

186

Through the dream-wake Mithos looked on, feeling a wave of revulsion take hold of him. He glanced at the wire-fronted cages. In them lay cats woozy after operations and dogs bleeding from dressed wounds. A spaniel with a bandaged tail and a cone around its neck pawed the wire, whining pitifully. Mithos edged back. Only humans could concoct such peculiar torture.

The prisoners in these cages could not see Mithos peering at them through the dream-wake. He moved freely, stalking down a corridor that smelled of disinfectant. He passed one cage after another but saw no sign of the sedicia. A human in a white jacket came striding toward him.

Mithos backed away into the shadow world on the boundaries of the dream-wake. "But he was here. . . . I sensed him . . . and he remains close even now," he hissed.

"Your senses do not deceive you." This was not the Suzerain's voice. But it was one Mithos knew, one loyal to the Suzerain and the Empire of Sa.

"Great Spirit Alia?"

"Yes, it is I. Your master has asked me to guide you. You are close now. Step forward."

Mithos slunk toward the cages.

"No. This way. Look for me."

Mithos turned, stared out through Fiåney, leaning into the voice, looking for the queen who had spoken. Instead, he saw the path to Mati sprawl ahead of him like a black river, the sleeping catling rising at its end, ruddy fur tinged

187

with flecks of light. Mithos stared through narrowed yellow eyes. A satisfied hiss escaped his parted lips through clenched teeth. "At last . . ." he gasped. He slunk back into the shadows where he could watch without being seen.

"Hunted in two realms by the same hunter," said the Suzerain. "You have done well, Mithos. You have found the sedicia twice: he is close in the land of flesh and fur, vulnerable, unaware. And in Fiåney he is nothing more than a lost wanderer in an endless maze. Tell me, in which world do you plan to finish him?"

Mati's body lay just beyond the clinic in the house next door, curled in a basket, his head resting against his paws. Mati's second self was even closer, wandering the labyrinths of Fiåney, blindly glancing this way and that, just beyond the reach of Mithos's arched claws.

Beyond the
Dream-Wake

The little red cat's whiskers trembled in his sleep.

"Are you dreaming, puss?" said the vet. She gently touched his forehead, then changed his drip. "I wonder. Chasing imaginary mice, perhaps?"

She switched on the television and drew her feet up onto the sofa, leaving him to his slumber.

Mati looked out through mists of sleep. Shapes quivered against layers of darkness. He stepped into the dream-wake, into the halls of Fiåney, as if stepping into a sunset. Basking in a warm pink light, he felt close to his mother, closer than he could remember. "I know you are near, Amma."

"You have sensed me," she said. "Your instincts are strong. This is the first pillar." She looked at him with golden eyes, so similar to the eyes of Te Bubas, so similar to his own eyes.

He ached to touch her. But there was no touch in the dream-wake. "I ignored the second pillar, Amma! My judgment failed, even after the spirit Bayo told me to remember the pillars, even after everything! I thought it was you out on the road, yet at the same time I also knew it wasn't. . . . Something has been wrong for a while. . . . I sensed it when the robin died . . . perhaps even before." Broken thoughts and phrases tripped through Mati's mind.

"You were tricked."

"Someone is trying to hurt me, Amma! I think . . ."

"Yes, child?"

"I think whoever it is also took you. You said I had to start a new life and then . . . then you left me. I thought you had abandoned me. I realize now you were trying to protect me." His voice was as clear and brittle as metal striking rock.

"I thought I could protect you," she said, "but I've failed. I underestimated my enemies. That is all in the past. Now they are your enemies, and you must look to your future to defeat them. You will need to step back into the waking world. Look!"

Mati watched in amazement. Rising before the image of his mother he saw a small ruddy cat curled in a basket, sleeping peacefully. He squinted through the dream-wake. "It's me!" he gasped. He stretched out a nervous paw to touch the sleeper, but he was just out of reach. He stepped forward, tried again, his paw swiping through air. "It's like trying to touch the moon. Right in front of my nose, but . . . I don't understand!"

"It's your first self. Your physical self. Safe for now. But soon you must find your way back to your body. Do you see the path?"

Mati's first self suddenly seemed far away, so faint he could hardly see him. The path between them was a black, winding river. It reminded Mati of the swollen waters of Cressida Lock. Of something else too. A river from his kittenhood, huge and endless. Mati shuddered. "I would rather stay here with you, Amma." The black river dissolved as he spoke; the figure of his first self vanished from view.

"My child, you must return to the waking world and defeat our enemies. You must leave this place to save yourself. Do you know where you are?"

"This is the place the shalian took me to, isn't it? This is the dream-wake, the spirit world?"

"That is right, my child. And didn't Etheleldra tell you that it is dangerous to stay here too long, that the mazes of Fiåney are endless, that you might never find your way out? Didn't she warn you that forces hostile to all we believe in prowl the borders of your dreams? You are not safe here."

"What difference does it make? What difference does it make if I live or die?" Self-pity distorted the shapes and colors of the dream-wake. Pink light deepened into red.

"It makes all the difference in the world."

"I don't see why. I don't see why the world would miss another stray cat. . . ."

"Because there is no such thing as 'another stray cat,'" sighed Mati's mother.

"Really, Amma?"

"Really. But it is not the only reason. Because you are my son . . . because of a promise I once made to some friends, a promise I honor through you, through your life. If you die, they will be left defenseless. The Sa will—" she broke off.

"Amma . . . ?"

"It is worse even than that. I fear no corner of this world will be worth living in for our kind."

"I don't understand . . ."

"I will show you what difference your life makes, what a world you would leave for your feline friends. Soon you will confront the dark. You will not like what you see . . ." Already her voice was fading, the light of sunset diminishing with the radiance of her golden eyes.

"Please, Amma. I'm scared of the dark! I don't dare confront it!" Fear replaced self-pity, fear followed by a jolt of shame.

When she replied, his mother's voice was as high and thin as wind through grass. "You must confront your terror. I cannot protect you. To cast a light in your darkest hour, simply speak your self."

Mati cried out for his mother. He felt himself falling

down a tunnel, as narrow and dark as the catacombs at Cressida Lock, but plunging through the center of the earth. He felt his stomach lurch and colors play at the corners of his vision. Two gray towers formed the shape of cherry trees, their bare branches bowing slightly in the breeze. Weathered narrow boats lay like dozing crocodiles by a riverbank. Some distance from the bank, on a stall overlooking a marketplace, sat a black tom with a limp tail. The tom seemed to look through Mati without seeing him.

"Pangur?" said Mati.

The black tom turned away to stare across the marketplace.

Mati's mind wandered along Cressida Lock. Everything looked the same as he'd remembered it. The hinds chatted excitedly at the stalls, the first hint of a spring sun playing across their faces. But the market was immediately alien, too, for the cats had changed. There was Arabella, the beautiful white Persian with that superior look on her face, only it wasn't superior anymore. She sat on the cobbles near the edge of the market square. She seemed lost.

Sparrow sheltered under the cherry trees. It was a familiar scene. Sparrow had always preferred this spot. And yet . . . it wasn't Sparrow, or the Sparrow that Mati had known. His good-natured smile had vanished. A small string of drool escaped his mouth to roll down his chin. It was unbearable to see him like this.

"Sparrow? Sparrow?" called Mati.

The great ginger looked up. Suddenly Mati realized what was wrong with him, what was wrong with all of them. Their eyes were blank. Brilliant green had been replaced by shadows.

Mati gave a small cry. He thought of Jess, and the thought was enough to conjure her image. He saw her padding toward a bowl in an unknown kitchen. She stood for a few moments without moving. Then, absently, she ate.

"She's eating! I think she's enjoying it! She's not like the others!" Mati's mind flooded with hope.

Jess stopped eating. She turned to him, slowly. She looked through him. The expression was one he was coming to recognize: blank, shaded eyes. He called to her but she didn't hear him. Her body lived and yet . . . he didn't recognize her face.

Mati was choked with panic. His mind stumbled away from the halls of Fiåney, into the surrounding shadows. From those shadows, yellow eyes flashed at him. Mati glanced into those eyes and saw, as if through his mother's eyes on her last night on earth, bitterness without boundary, untiring malice.

Far away in the waking world, in the basket once owned by a cat called Paws, Mati's body shook with fear. Summoning his courage, he stepped back into Fiåney. The yellow eyes had gone but a rancid smell remained, like rotten eggs. The eyes were close, haunting him from a land beyond dreams.

Mati took a step farther into the dream-wake. The air was thick. Distorted voices from unknown chanters encircled him:

> Ha'atta, Ha'atta!
> Te Bubas, we call to you
> Your one true heir stands before you
> We do your bidding
> Lords on earth
> Spirits of the Sa are we
> Messengers of your legacy . . .

It was very dark, almost black. The chanting faded. Mati began to relax. His vision adjusted to the darkness, splashing a thin light before him. It was then that he realized he wasn't alone.

Sitting some paces away was a fine-boned cat with spots on his arched back like a leopard's. His black eyes seemed to suck up light like strange black holes. They reflected nothing. He turned to look at Mati. A single word, no more than a hiss, spilled from his mouth. *"Sssaaaaaa."*

Suddenly Mati felt it: the light wrenched from him, a pang in his chest. Color bled from shapes, leaving only smudges of darkness. He tried to howl, but terror snared his voice. He started falling again, a tearing pain as the light faded. Mati was sinking, but something else was happening to him. From somewhere unexpected, a rebellious force in

Mati lunged toward the vanishing light. "It was you who took my amma!" he cried, thrashing his paws, claws unsheathed. "It was you who tricked me onto the road! You'd take the fur from my back! You'd steal the light from my eyes! You won't have it; I won't let you!"

Mati's voice faded from the halls of Fiåney as he fell deeper, deeper into vaults of sleep. But something came with him from the dream-wake: a gentle light that sank with Mati into folds of darkness, into tunnels of sleep without dreams.

The old man was speaking to his daughter on the telephone. Jess paced around the kitchen. She had hardly eaten in the days since he had told her about the ancient cats. She paused near the cat door and washed herself distractedly. She was thinking about that look she had noticed on Mati's face once or twice—a faraway look, as if his mind were on other more important things. With that look, his eyes seemed to glow.

She wanted the old man to tell her more about the ancient cats, but there was probably no hope of that now. Once a subject was forgotten, there was no guessing how long it might take him to recall it. Perhaps never. Humans were tricky like that. Jess paced back into the study.

The old man was at his desk, clutching the telephone receiver. "Children are so territorial. That bully is unlikely to give up until he owns half the street. . . . I know, but there isn't that much that can be done, not with his mentality. It's obvious the parents don't know how to control him. . . . Yes, yes, I realize that. It's just unfortunate that he's also in Hannah's class. . . . Well, of course you could move her to a different school, but he'd still be a neighbor, wouldn't he? And he'd have won, in a way. . . . Certainly not—I'd never suggest that Hannah should just 'put up with it'!"

Jess sat in her usual spot by the radiator. She contemplated what her old man had said: "That bully is unlikely to give up . . ." For some reason, this comment struck her. She thought of the death of the first robin of the harvest moon and how the Cressida Cats had turned on Mati. She thought of the flood. She thought again about how unusual Mati was: his appearance, his unique instincts, his strange arrival by ship. Finally, she thought about the battle between two feline tribes ten thousand years ago.

She turned to the window, beyond the sculpture of Bastet that so resembled Mati. The sky was clearer than it had been in days, and sunlight streamed between the clouds.

"Perhaps next weekend," continued the old man. "I want to stay in the house as much as possible as Jess readjusts. . . . Don't be like that; you know she's not 'just a cat' to me. The poor thing is so skinny. I've been trying to fatten her up, but she hasn't had much of an appetite. . . . Sunday lunch next week? I'd be delighted to come. But there's nothing to stop you from coming here this week. . . ."

Jess drew her eyes away from the window. The book on ancient Egypt was sitting on the floor by the old man's feet.

It was a large, dog-eared volume, probably opened too many times, and several pages didn't lie flat. On one of the curling, upward-facing pages Jess saw a splash of what looked like reddish fur. She crept closer, ears flattened. She reached into the book with a curved paw and pressed down the page. The picture showed a cat. One side of its face was bony and spotted, with a staring eye. The other side . . . Jess shook her head slowly.

She thought about the ancient rivalry that had led to a massive feline battle ten thousand years ago. Jess did not understand how, or why, but she was suddenly sure that the feud had not run its course. Somehow, Mati was involved . . . was more than involved: he was in danger.

Jess glanced out of the window again. Already the faintest hint of a silvery dusk touched the sky.

How far away was the marketplace? she wondered. How would she find it? Her old man had told her he would never understand how she had made it so far west as the river. West. *That's the direction of the sunset*, thought Jess. At the end of the sunset, she would find the marketplace. Once darkness fell, she would lose her compass. It was late afternoon. She didn't have much time.

The old man continued to chat on the telephone. "Yes, but spring is on the way, I feel it. . . . So I'm an optimist!"

Jess refused to look at him. She walked out of the room and slunk through the cat door in the kitchen.

Perhaps the old man heard this, as something made him hesitate.

"Dad? Dad?" his daughter's voice boomed out of the receiver.

The old man made his excuses and got off the telephone. It made no difference. Jess was already beyond the fence at the back of the garden and running away as quickly as she could.

Battle Song

Truth and vengeance, tit-for-tat
When you take on a Cressida Cat!

Singing their rallying song, the Cressida Cats fell into step behind their chief. Pangur led his kin at a steady pace, tail raised high.

Every cat fit to march followed close behind. Every cat, that is, except Binjax, who had been told to stand guard over the catacombs. He hung back, scowling, his eyes slits, his tail twitching.

"Ever since the flood, it's as if I'm a second-class citizen on the market I was born to rule," he hissed under his breath as the Cressida Cats marched onward.

Twilight sank over Cressida Lock. A low moon, almost full, rose before them. Pangur paused as they reached the tall iron railings of the park. The rallying song faded. The ferals whispered among themselves.

Pangur turned to address them. "We Cressida Cats usually avoid this park. There's a reason. The Kanks live just beyond it." The ferals chorused their agreement in hisses and boos. "It has been our practice to leave them alone, to stay safe within the boundaries of the Territory. This has been an unspoken agreement between two communities of ferals, an agreement sealed in mutual honor.

"But some moons ago, this agreement was broken. By my brother, and Kank leader, Hanratty!" The hisses grew louder, more impassioned. "That agreement now being broken, we will march upon the Kanks. We will show them what it is to cross a Cressida Cat!" Cheers, whoops, caterwauls. Pangur slid under the iron bars, followed by his kin.

The ferals knew this was only part of the story. There was another reason the cats avoided the park. Haunted, some called it. Ria drew level with Domino. They exchanged nervous glances.

Domino turned to his mother, who marched behind him. "Did I make a mistake?" he asked quietly.

"No, son. You did the right thing by telling me, just as we're doing the right thing now. Sometimes there is no alternative but to confront your enemies. This is such a time. Did we go to the Kanks, plotting and scheming?"

"No, Amma."

"Exactly. They started it. They left us with no choice."

Domino nodded and turned back to Pangur, who had passed flower beds from which the first daffodils would soon bloom. With bold steps, Pangur advanced over the lawn where Mati had found the hollow oak on the night of the flood. Two robins fluttered through the air, locked in combat. They tumbled and dived before darting between the branches of a horse chestnut tree. Pangur glanced back at his old friend Trillion. None of the Cressida Cats spoke.

The cats trod carefully through the deserted park, strangely subdued. They headed north, where lawns gave way to thorny weeds. At the far border of the park, the ferals scrambled under a bramble bush. Out in a courtyard, gathering under a flickering streetlamp, Pangur and his kin drew to a halt. It was growing late. Not a single human was in sight. It wasn't much of a territory, certainly nothing to rival Cressida Lock. The courtyard had once been grand, overlooked by an imposing Victorian library. In the center stood a disused bandstand where, long ago, men in white suits with silver buttons and starched hats had blown trumpets and beaten drums. Their proud fanfares had captivated crowds of spectators.

Not anymore. The bandstand was deserted, the stone edges streaked white from pigeon droppings. The once-imposing Victorian library had since been condemned as a health risk. Ugly scaffolding pinned it together. A blue tarpaulin hanging against the scaffolding had come loose at one corner, slapping the brickwork with each jolt of wind.

The Cressida Cats gathered on steps that trailed down to the courtyard. Domino and Ria huddled together, exchanging worried glances. The blue tarpaulin edged away from the scaffolding. A small gray cat pounced onto the tarmac.

Domino turned to Trillion. "It's him, Amma! He's the one I saw at the marketplace!"

Trillion nodded. The Cressida Cats looked on as, one by one, Kanks spilled from gaps behind the tarpaulin, collecting at the foot of the building. Pangur watched steadily, his face blank. He didn't flinch when the last cat to emerge, a black tom very like himself, sprang onto the paving to sit before his kin.

The cat looked directly at Pangur with the same green eyes. "Well, well, brother," said the black tom.

"Well, well, Hanratty," said Pangur.

Nobody moved. The Kanks and the Cressida Cats watched nervously. At length, Pangur stood up in an unhurried sort of way, twisting sideways to Hanratty, maintaining eye contact throughout. The chief of the Kanks at the far end of the courtyard did the same.

"I know it was you at Cressida Lock. You plotted to overthrow us," began Pangur. A hiss rose from his kin, but he silenced it with a flick of his tail. "Tell me, what methods did you use to 'urge' the fishmonger to open the lock? I suppose you baited him? Perhaps you mewled in front of his door every night? Perhaps you goaded him at his stall?"

"It wasn't hard," spat Hanratty. "Hinds are stupid! They're

easy to control. It didn't take much."

A hint of a frown crossed Pangur's face. He inched forward, still sideways to Hanratty, toward the low bandstand in the middle of the courtyard.

Hanratty mirrored him, taking a small step closer.

"You have courted disaster at Cressida Lock. Now we return it to *your* territory," said Pangur. His paws stayed in the same place, but his body lowered toward the ground, an action copied by Hanratty.

Both chiefs fell silent for a moment. Their kins were quiet. The blue tarpaulin smacked the scaffolding.

The brothers stared along the side of the bandstand, their eyes locked. Neither blinked. The Kanks and the Cressida Cats watched, hardly daring to breathe.

Pangur was the first to make a sound—a low "Hisssssssss!"

This was immediately echoed by Hanratty: "Hisssssssss!"

After a few moments, Pangur gave a "Mmmeeeeeeooooow!"

"Mmmeeeeeeeeoooooooow!" replied Hanratty.

Slowly, Pangur rose to his full height. Every hair on his body puffed up and his whiskers strained forward. When he spoke, his voice had risen in pitch and volume. "I am the chief of the Cressida Cats, and I order you to surrender!"

The Kanks and the Cressida Cats watched in tense silence. Hanratty froze for several seconds. Then he, too, rose to his full height. "I am the chief of the Kanks, and I do not surrender! You are a trespasser on our territory: you will bow to the Kanks!" Several of his kin echoed their agreement, but nobody moved.

"Very well," said Pangur quietly. The older among the assembled ferals stiffened, knowing what would follow. Pangur took one step forward and, in a high-pitched whine, began to sing:

> *The Cressida Cats have long possessed*
> *The marketplace at Cressida Lock*
> *Invaders cannot breach its walls*
> *Without a deathly shock*

Hanratty took one step forward and made this reply:

> *Each stall that stands at Cressida Lock,*
> *The river and the grassy banks*
> *The cherry trees, the catacombs*
> *Belong now to the Kanks*

Pangur took two steps forward, which brought him to the base of the bandstand. He sang the next phrase of his fugue in a shrill voice:

> *We offered you a noble truce*
> *Though we can fight with tooth and claw*
> *You fail to bow before our might*
> *So must prepare for war!*

With that, Pangur sprang up onto the edge of the empty bandstand. For a moment, Hanratty seemed to hesitate. The Cressida and Kank kins edged forward, necks craned. Seeming to make his up mind, Hanratty took two steps forward:

No Kank will bow before a fool:
Our honor must be kept
To mortify our feeble foe
And therefore, we accept!

Hanratty's tail twitched slightly. He drew in his breath. And then he jumped onto the bandstand.

The vet zapped channels on the television with the remote control. She yawned. "Time for bed," she announced to no one in particular.

Nearby, in the wicker basket, a small mound of reddish fur slept. His whiskers trembled. The shapes of Fiåney were shifting, fading. Someone was calling to him.

"Do you hear me, Mati? This is Bayo. I am a spirit. Do you remember me? We spoke before in Etheleldra's hollow oak. It is time for you to wake up. You have been in Fiåney too long. Your amma has warned you: it is no longer safe for you here. A shadow draws over your first self. You must find your way back to your body before he does. You must wake up. You must wake up. . . ."

There was a rap at the door. Not really a rap—more a slow, scratching sound.

Suspecting another casualty of the roads, the vet walked past the sleeping cat into the well-lit hall and leaned up against the spy hole.

Mati shifted in his sleep, but he didn't awaken.

"Mati, you must hear me! You must wake up! Wake up!"

The porch outside was dark. The vet placed the safety chain on the door and opened it a few inches. "Hello?"

No reply.

Her eyes scanned the porch. The gate leading to her small front garden swung gently on its hinges. She glanced at the hedge where honeysuckle grew in summer. In the silvery light, its edges looked as sharp as claws. Pools of shadow gathered around the hedge. The vet closed the door, took off the safety chain and opened it again, more widely this time. She stepped out onto the porch.

Definitely no one there. A motorbike howled as it whizzed by on the street. A dog barked not far away. She started to close the door.

In the shadows around the hedge, there was a rustling. The vet squinted. A hedgehog, perhaps? No, it was only March; hedgehogs would still be hibernating. A low hiss made her start. Huge yellow eyes flashed at her. The faintest hint of a vile smell, like rotten eggs.

The vet slammed the door shut and bolted it, her heart racing. She backed into the hall. "Definitely time for bed," she said aloud, banishing the dark with her voice. She started toward the stairs.

Then, remembering, she headed back toward the living room and switched off the television. A draft cooled the hairs on the back of her neck. With surprise, the vet realized that the window was slightly ajar, the curtain fluttering against it. She shut the window, turned back toward the room. The wicker basket caught her eye. The feeding drip dangled loosely against the basket. From this angle it looked as if . . .

The vet drew closer, dropping to her knees. Frowning, she looked inside the basket.

It was empty.

To Cast a Light

An almost full moon floated above the low clouds that hung over the marketplace. The cobbles underfoot were cool, the air clammy. Jess stood for a moment, regaining her breath. She had run flat out until nightfall, chasing the vanishing sun to the riverbank upstream, careful to take in sights and smells along the way, to keep her bearings. From there, she had hastened alongside the snaking river until it finally led her to Cressida Lock. To do what? To warn the ferals. Of what, exactly?

"Mati," she said aloud. She had to find Mati. The marketplace was strangely deserted. No night prowlers hunting rodents, no amorous toms and queens. Jess approached the cherry trees and the entrance to the catacombs and stumbled into Binjax, who seemed shocked to see her.

"What are you doing back?"

"Never mind that," returned Jess. "I need to find Mati. There's something important I have to tell him."

Binjax's ears flicked back. "You can't—"

"Don't start, Binjax. I'm not in the mood!" Jess interrupted. She walked around him toward the catacombs.

"No—I mean Mati's not here."

Jess swung around. "Where is he?"

Binjax hesitated. "He . . . he had an accident. On the road . . . He's not been back."

"What?" Jess's face fell. "He can't have! You're lying! You always were a nasty little liar!"

"It's true," said Binjax. "Domino was with him. . . . Seems he ran onto the road—Domino couldn't stop him."

"Why would he do that? It doesn't make sense!"

Binjax shifted uncomfortably. "I don't know. . . . But he's not here, so you're wasting your time looking for him."

"But . . . but he's alive, isn't he?" Jess and Binjax avoided each other's eyes. "Where's everyone else? Pangur? Domino? Where are they?"

"Fighting the Kanks."

"*What?*"

"Long story . . . Turns out the Kanks caused all that trouble with the fishmonger. Hanratty is Pangur's brother; he wanted to take over the marketplace."

Jess glanced toward the river, distracted. "I don't care about that!" she snapped. "Where are they all?"

"The courtyard beyond the park. Where the Kanks—"

"What's that smell, for heaven's sake?"

Binjax blinked at her, surprised. "What smell?"

"Can't you smell it? I thought I smelled something awful, like rotten eggs."

Binjax concentrated a moment, then nodded. "I don't know. . . . I hadn't noticed it before."

"If you see Mati, warn him!" Jess turned toward the park.

"Warn him about what?" asked Binjax.

Jess didn't reply. She ran as quickly as she could to the iron railings, crawled beneath them, and disappeared into the park.

Binjax sniffed the air and looked about. A sharp wind seemed to rise from nowhere, stirring the buds on the cherry trees, making him shiver.

Jess sprinted across the park, mindless of the rats that scattered with angry squeaks. She made for the bramble patch at the north of the park, scrambling under to emerge at the Kanks' courtyard, where caterwauls filled the air.

Pangur and Hanratty were crouched on the bandstand, their kins drawn close on the paving below, joining them in a threatening chorus of meows, howls, and curses. For a moment both leaders looked the same, but Jess noticed that Hanratty was slightly thinner, with a narrower face and shorter tail. Pangur and Hanratty stared at each other, eyes locked. Both had spots of blood clinging to their fur. Hanratty seemed the worse for wear, with one eye almost swollen shut.

"Pangur, Mr. Pangur, sir, I need to talk to you urgently!" blurted Jess, pressing between the Cressida Cats. Startled faces turned to her. For a moment, Pangur and Hanratty turned, too, their concentration broken.

"You!" said Pangur. "Go home to your hind, stray!" The Cressida Cats hissed their agreement, with some help from the Kanks.

Jess winced. "Please, Mr. Pangur, it's important. Mati is not who we thought he was, and he's in danger—"

"Mati?" said Sparrow, with sad eyes.

"Mati's not here," said Pangur. He turned back to Hanratty.

"I know, but . . . He'll come back. Where else could he go? There's a tribe called the Sa Mau—"

"What do you know about the Sa?" demanded Hanratty, turning to look at Jess as if seeing her for the first time.

"The Sa are a dark force—I don't really understand everything yet, but . . . but it will affect everything, somehow. The Sa had something to do with Mati's accident; I'm sure of it!"

"Rubbish!" cried Hanratty. "The Sa are eastern cats of wisdom and nobility. A messenger of the great Suzerain himself first advised me of the spoils at Cressida Lock."

Pangur turned to his brother in fury, green eyes flashing. "It was you watching me on that night. Watching after you had baited the fishmonger into opening the lock!"

"So what if it was?" hissed Hanratty. "The messenger of the Sa told me about the marketplace, and reminded me it was

212

my birthright. What makes my brother, older but by minutes, think he has the right to claim it as his own? What has this brother ever done for me? The messenger was right about the fishmonger, too. He was right about a lot of things. . . ."

The members of both kins watched their chiefs uneasily. Already Jess was forgotten in the face of these new revelations.

"Since when does my brother take orders from this Suzerain, this eastern despot?" growled Pangur.

"Since I realized where real power lies."

"What did the Sa promise you?" cried Jess. "All lies! Don't you see? You can't trust them! They're our worst side— they're the killer instinct that makes us turn on each other! There was a battle once, an ancient battle and . . . What I mean is that there's another tribe from the east, the Tyg—"

"You let this queen, this catling, this *stray* speak on your behalf?" Hanratty spat the words—especially "stray."

"No, I do not. I speak for myself, and for my kin," replied Pangur. "You have taken bribes from a foreign power—you are even more corrupt than I imagined. You will pay for this!" Pangur pounced on Hanratty, forelegs gripping his shoulders, back legs raking his belly. The two cats tumbled in a cloud of fur, claws, and blood.

"Listen to me," Jess pleaded. "Mati's in danger—we have to do something! Don't you see? It affects us, too!"

But they ignored her. The Cressida Cats and the Kanks, alarmed by the leap from ritual combat to all-out battle, turned back to the bandstand, where their leaders fought.

The defeat of either meant disaster for their kin: domination, expulsion, even death.

Mati wasn't quite sure how he'd found his way back to Cressida Lock. Somehow, his feet knew exactly where to go. He had been awoken by Bayo, the spirit he had talked to from Etheleldra's hollow oak. A good spirit, she had told him then. When Mati had opened his eyes in that strange house, his body had felt fit. But his instincts had somehow been damaged. *Run*, they had told him. *Danger is close.* The source of the danger was unclear. Without a home to return to, Mati had come here, to the marketplace overlooking a riverbank.

He arrived cautiously, his golden eyes drinking in the familiar sights: the distant river, the boarded-up church, the abandoned warehouse. His mind compared these images with those drawn from Fiåney, from the world of spirits and his own imagination. Dazed, he thought of Te Bubas and his mother, queens who shared his own red coat. With a wave of fear, Mati remembered the shadow-cat who had pursued him among folds of sleep, and the face of that cat's master beyond the shadow. Mati knew that these mysterious cats had been responsible, somehow, for his mother's death. They had wanted him, too. But why? The answer was so close he, could almost taste it. Almost . . .

But other thoughts were jostling for attention. If the shadow-cat had killed Mati's mother, then perhaps he could take physical form outside the dream-wake.

Which means he could be out there somewhere waiting for me! thought Mati. He glanced about nervously. The night was still. His mind strayed back to his struggle with the shadow-cat in Fiåney, how he'd thrashed and fought. Mati's ears flattened. Was it safe here, back at the marketplace? He couldn't be sure.

What has happened to my instincts? To my judgment? he thought. The signs were there, Mati felt certain of it, but he no longer knew how to read them. He became aware of a foul smell, like rotten eggs. More than simply the stench of the bins, it raised the hairs on the back of his neck. But what did it mean?

He started toward the cherry trees and paused. There was Binjax, looking away in the direction of the park. Mati drew back, making for the far end of the catacombs, near the lock. He hesitated, distracted by whispering voices that pressed against his ears, the urgent call of spirits from Fiåney. The voices blended together, like droplets of water in a stream, so that Mati was unable to understand them. Only the occasional word or phrase escaped, catching his attention.

"Away . . . third pillar . . . danger . . . to cast a light . . . darkness . . . behind you!"

Binjax took several steps closer, and Mati dashed under a stall, keen to avoid his enemy. Immediately, he gasped. The air under the stall was so sharp, it burned his throat. The smell of rotten eggs surrounded him in the darkness. He spun around, heart hammering against his ribs, and felt faint as he saw those yellow eyes.

"We have met before, Mati, but not in this world." The yellow eyes floated in front of him. Peering into them, Mati saw many ages of the moon. He saw bitterness without boundary, untiring malice.

"Mithos," murmured Mati. The name sprang to his lips without his ever having heard it. Mithos, his mother's assassin, the creature who had followed Mati from his desert home, where all life had once begun, had stalked him through the spirit world, and finally found him here. "A trap," said Mati. The pillars of instinct and judgment seemed to melt before him. Hadn't both let him down? A stab of rage ran through him, rage at the spirits for failing to protect him, failing to warn him.

"You escaped me in Fiåney," hissed Mithos. "You shall not escape me now!" His yellow eyes were acid. He sneered, flashing ivory teeth, teeth that could slice through skin and tissue, teeth that could shatter bone.

Rats' feet danced in Mati's stomach.

"Run, Mati!" cried a voice from Fiåney. His mother's voice? It jolted him out of his trance. He scrambled out from under the stall and sprinted past the cherry trees. Mithos sprang after him, the callused pads of his paws drumming against the cobbles, his overgrown claws scratching like wire on glass. He was huge, powerful, gaining on Mati with each step. Mati bolted across the market square and found himself at the site of the full-moon meeting. He leaped from stall to stall, up the side of the towering elm and onto the rooftop of the abandoned warehouse, descending along the guttering, down to the riverbank. Mati sprinted downstream, paws barely touching the cigarette butts and beer cans littering his way. He skidded on a candy wrapper, losing his footing. He had backed himself against a weeping willow, fur puffed up, gasping for breath.

Mithos stopped tail lengths away, sneering. "Where will you go now, kit? If you climb up the tree, I will follow you; I will drag you down by the tail. You are not worth a duel. I will take you quickly. By the throat. Do you want that? Or do you crave a warrior's death? We can fight if you like— would you like *that*?"

Mati shook his head. He couldn't speak. Panic had flooded his brain. *I'm trapped! I'm trapped!* he thought in terror.

White spots formed at the corners of his vision. Broken phrases strained to be heard. His mother's voice: "To cast a light . . . To cast a light . . ." The voice faded.

Mithos dived at him, his claw scraping Mati's throat. Mati's head crashed against the tree with a *THUMP!* and violet shadows drew over his eyes.

Pangur leaped toward Hanratty, but something happened midleap, causing him to jerk violently and collapse against his brother on the bandstand. Hanratty's eyes were already clenched shut, garbled words spluttering from his tongue.

Jess looked to the surrounding ferals of the Cressida and Kank kins. One by one, their faces became contorted with pain, confusion, and fear. She saw Domino whimpering, fallen onto his side, his legs kicking feebly. Then she felt it, like a physical blow, a terrible desperate grief that wrapped itself around her throat. With a small cry, Jess doubled over, stunned by her sorrow.

At the same moment, house cats curled on beds or stalking country gardens were struck by an overpowering despair. Humans awoke to their yowling pets, writhing on carpets from bloodless wounds, clawing and mewling pitifully. "Help us! Help us!" they seemed to cry. Kittens and wise old queens, tough toms and pampered pedigrees— they all felt unbearable anguish.

Leaning next to the bandstand in the Kanks' courtyard, Jess closed her eyes. Something was being wrenched from inside her, something dear to her, a sort of inner light. The pain of losing it was worse than anything she could imagine. Gasping, she opened her eyes to find Pangur watching her.

He was trying to speak, but the words wouldn't come. With enormous effort, the black tom inched closer until his whiskers were almost touching hers. He spoke in an agonized whisper. "What's . . . happening . . . to . . . us?"

Jess shuddered, replied faintly, "Mati . . . The Sa . . ."

Pangur nodded, raising his head with difficulty.

Just as suddenly as the terrible sensation had started, it

vanished. The aftershock left the ferals trembling and confused. They glanced at each other, ears flat and eyes wild.

Pangur drew himself up. "Cats of Cressida Lock," he said, voice quivery. "The small reddish cat called Mati is somewhere on the marketplace. . . . Whoever the Sa is, whatever the Sa is, it's harming Mati. He's in trouble and . . . and so, therefore, are we."

The cats looked from one to the other, struggling to understand what this meant. Hanratty shook his head slowly.

"What just happened? And what's it got to do with Mati?" gasped Trillion.

"Jess was right. Even though it hardly makes sense. . . . Don't you feel it, too? That it is Mati who guards us from the terrible emptiness that we all just felt, that nothing will protect us if he dies? Our strength returns as his does. Is that right?" These questions were directed at Jess.

"Yes, I think so," she agreed.

"We must find Mati," Pangur continued. "We must find him *now*."

Trillion nodded. Clumsily, Pangur sprang off the bandstand. Jess and the Cressida Cats fell in behind him, stumbling as fast as they were able toward the bramble bush at the verge of the courtyard.

"Aren't you forgetting something?" asked Hanratty. He stood awkwardly on the bandstand, one eye swollen shut and his fur ragged. Pangur turned, tensing for a fight. Hanratty glanced at his kin. He breathed heavily, and gradually his claws slid back into his paws. He cleared his throat. "You are forgetting *us*. We will help you." He jumped down after Pangur. "This Mati must be found, and his enemy defeated. By helping the Sa, I had no idea . . . We have been tricked. You may add our number to your army."

Pangur nodded, smiled faintly. He opened his mouth, but for a moment he said nothing. Then he murmured, "Thank you, brother." Together, they led their kins under the bramble bush.

Mati opened his eyes, and color flooded back. Mithos had loosened his grip, was stumbling backward slightly. Binjax was locked around his neck.

"Run, Mati—I can't hold him," gasped Binjax.

"You!" cried Mati, bewildered to find his sworn enemy helping him.

"I owe you, don't I? Now get out of here!"

Mati leaped to his feet, bolting toward the cherry trees and into the maze of the catacombs. Mithos growled and gave a powerful jerk of the neck, throwing Binjax into the surrounding shrubs. Binjax looked up, winded.

"Fool! You think you can hold me?" Mithos gave a low rasping laugh. "No one can hold me." He turned toward the catacombs, his bitter stench wafting about him.

Binjax watched helplessly, struggling to regain his breath.

As Mithos reached the mouth of the catacombs, Binjax raised the alarm—a long, screeching yowl.

Deep inside the catacombs, Mati heard only a faint whine. He sprang down dark passages, immediately lost, his only instinct to run. Then he heard it, the scratch of Mithos's long claws on the tunnel floor, faint at first, but gaining on him. Mati scrambled through a narrow door where no full-grown cat would be able to pass to a broad opening buried underground. The air was tired and thin. In the distance he heard a shuffling, paws thumping and, finally, the scratching of long, brittle claws against the narrow door. Panic coursed through Mati's body in sharp stabs. He swallowed hard, focused on regaining his senses, on honing his instincts. He waited in silence until the scratching stopped. His whiskers bristled; his ears flattened.

Mithos fell silent on the far side of the door. Then Mati heard a low chanting that set his hairs on end:

Ha'atta, Ha'atta! Sa can see through
Harakar, Harakar, draw us to you
Draw us backward, draw us inward
Darkness, Harakar, chaos, Harakar

He's going to enter Fiåney! thought Mati desperately. *He's going to try to find me there like he did before!*

In moments, Mati felt the dream-wake calling to him, whispering in his ears, humming against his paws. Heat rose from the floor of the chamber. In the dream-wake, no wall could hold Mithos, no physical laws could control him. He would slip through the door and take hold of Mati in a moment; he would be unstoppable. Even though Mati sensed this, his thoughts began to unravel. He felt himself sinking into the space before sleep, on the journey toward dreams.

No! thought Mati. *I won't enter Fiåney with him waiting for me — he won't drag me there!*

Mati jerked awake, shook his head forcefully, and found that the humming from his paws had vanished and the voices from the dream-wake were silent. Silent, too, was Mithos, no longer chanting, back in the physical realm. Over the sound of his own pounding heart, Mati could sense the tom's frustration in the oaths and curses that rose in his throat but never emerged as words, the anger crackling like static from his fur.

It's hopeless, thought Mati dismally. *He'll never give up. Whether here or in Fiåney, he'll chase me forever.*

Eventually, Mati heard the low, brassy thump of Mithos's paws on the floor of the catacombs, fading away. Mati squinted into the dark chamber. He started crawling under the low ceiling, searching for another way out.

Mithos appeared by the cherry trees as the Cressida and Kank kins arrived on the marketplace. The ferals froze, some forty cats standing in a semicircle. The stranger sat watching them, larger than any normal cat, his fur pale, tan marks like liver spots dappling his back. His face was bony with bulging yellow eyes. Danger and power rose from him in sharp waves. There was cruelty etched around his mouth, an expression between a sneer and a threatening smile. The two chiefs, Pangur and Hanratty, exchanged anxious glances.

For a moment, nobody spoke. A darkness blacker than any night sky enclosed the marketplace. With the darkness came a pungent smell like rotten eggs, and an eerie stillness.

The silence was broken by Binjax, who ran toward Pangur, glanced in confusion at Hanratty, then fell before them both. "He's after Mati!"

"Where is Mati?" pressed Domino, taking a step toward Binjax, keeping Mithos in his eye line.

"I don't know," said Binjax quietly.

He was about to say something else when Mithos announced in a commanding voice, "I am the servant of the Suzerain. I represent the cats of the Sa Mau. I am here to claim the red cat." There was an electricity in his voice that startled the ferals and set their teeth chattering.

"Why?" asked Pangur. No one dared say more.

"Because he has no right to exist, because his existence represents a betrayal to the Sa. Step aside!"

None of the ferals moved. Mithos laughed, a rough, hollow sound that raised their fur on end. "Nothing but house cats gone wild, living like beggars on the fringes of hind society. The Master is right: this depravity must end, and soon it shall. You disgust me, but today my fight is not with you. You will step aside. You will step aside or be killed!"

"Do you see our number? Who do you think you are?" said Hanratty, anger freeing his tongue.

"I am the servant of the Suzerain, the one true lord of cats, and I will see my duty done. Step aside or be killed," repeated Mithos. He didn't raise his voice.

"You will not come to our territories and order us to step aside. Mati is a member of our kin, and only we may decide his fate," said Pangur.

"Now get out, before we rip out your tongue for your insolence!" growled Hanratty. He started pacing toward the intruder with sudden rage.

"Over, around, or through you. It makes no difference," hissed Mithos. In a flash, before the ferals knew what was happening, he had darted the distance from the cherry trees and had Hanratty by the throat.

A moment later, the chief of the Kanks lay limp at his feet.

"You will die for this!" cried Pangur.

"No!" begged Jess, pawing him. "No, he'll kill you, too!"

Pangur turned to Jess. "He was my brother."

"I know," said Jess. "But we need you, Pangur, now more than ever. Both kins need you."

"Coward!" cried the small gray from the Kank kin, loyal to Hanratty, directing his grief at Pangur. "If you don't defend your brother's honor, let me at least remember our leader!"

"Block him!" ordered Pangur, and several of the ferals closest to the gray closed around him.

But in moments the gray had scrambled free and was running headlong toward Mithos with a high-pitched shriek. Mithos made a dive for him and flung him to the ground. The ferals glanced at each other in horror.

"You may pick us off one by one," shouted Pangur. "But you will not take us together! You have intruded upon our feral community—you call us house cats gone wild. Sir, you underestimate us! Every one of us is a fighter, and together we are more than the sum of our parts! Is that not so, Kanks?" Pangur turned to the Kank kin to his right. "Is that not so, Cressida Cats?" He gave a nod to the cats on his left. "Prepare to strike!" he ordered.

The ferals stiffened. Mithos stood watching, a grim smile playing on his lips. *Do your worst*, it seemed to say. *I will still defeat you.*

Pangur gave the nod, and the ferals charged, a semicircle closing around Mithos. In a moment, cats were thrown to the ground, one after the other.

"He'll kill us all, until there's no one left!" cried Fink, watching another cat fall.

"He's invincible! No one can touch him!" wailed Ria.

"Stop!" The voice rang out across the marketplace. "Enough blood has been spilled in my name." Mati stood on the cobbles, his russet fur pressed down by the chilly night wind.

Mithos froze. The ferals fell back.

"Don't let Mati be touched! If he dies, we all die!" cried Trillion.

"You won't die—but you won't really be alive, either," said Mati. "I've seen it in the dream-wake. This cat means to steal your spirit, your second self. He and his leader. Your second self is what gives you the light in your eyes; it's what makes you who you are. I didn't even know it existed before, but it's always there. The shalian told me, and I've come to understand it better in Fiâney. It's invisible, but I know it exists. I learned what a cat becomes without it: just a sort of shell. Spirit is what gives us all meaning; it's what makes us make sense." Mati turned to Mithos. "It's also the third pillar."

Mithos opened his mouth as if to speak, then closed it again.

Mati stared at him, struggling against every instinct that told him to run. "You thought I didn't know about the pillars," he said.

"It makes no difference. It is too late for you." Mithos spoke directly to Mati, indifferent to the ferals scattered around him.

Mati's hairs stood up like sharp little needles, and his breath came short. But his gaze was steady.

"Don't let him get Mati! We're all doomed!" cried Arabella, but the other ferals had fallen silent. Even the pitiful whimpers of scared and wounded cats were stilled under the distant moon.

Mati struggled to focus his mind on Mithos. "It took a long time to understand what I am, and what you are, but now I sense it. . . ."

Mithos took a step closer. "Your amma sensed it too, and it did not save her," he hissed.

Mati swallowed a furious cry. "She died protecting me. . . ."

"Then she died for nothing." Mithos took another step closer, low to the ground like a stalking leopard.

Mati strained his ears to hear Mithos. The stillness of the night was disturbed by the voices of spirits. Some were issuing orders such as "Run" or "Fight"; some were speaking in an ancient tongue that he couldn't understand. Was his mother's voice among them?

Concentrate, he told himself. *It's your last chance.* Mati remembered the quiet of Etheleldra's oak and willed himself there. He closed his eyes. Heat was rising from his paws.

And there she was—Mati's mother—still beautiful, smiling at him, calling his name. "You cannot fight him. You cannot escape him. You must cast your light." The voice faded; the face dissolved.

Mati opened his eyes. Mithos was standing only tail lengths away. Mati looked into those bitter yellow eyes without flinching. At their dark center he saw the other figure, the cat behind the shadow, the Suzerain, waiting for news of Mati's death. Mati spoke, as if to himself, a mumbled whisper. "To cast a light in your darkest hour, simply speak yourself. . . . *Yourself*? Or was that your *self*? *My self*?"

The ferals inched closer, watching Mati with desperation. Jess alone hung back, brows furrowed, trying to understand what her old man had told her, to put it all together.

"I am Mati," said the little ruddy cat. Nothing happened. Mati recalled Te Bubas from the dream-wake. What had she asked him? *And who are you?* He had said "Mati" then, too, and the first cat had seemed disappointed.

"It's something to do with where you came from!" shouted Jess. "Something to do with Nubia, or the two kittens of the first cat. There was a battle once, a huge battle; I think you may be—" She broke off. Mithos had craned his neck to stare at her. Under his gaze she shrank in terror, unable to utter another word.

Triumphantly, Mithos turned back to Mati.

Mati glanced frantically at Jess, at the ferals. *It's too late,* he thought. *He's got me—I've failed.* Suddenly he was impossibly tired, a sort of aching weariness from deep within his bones. He felt no anger, not even fear, just an unbearable sense of sadness. His head drooped, and he shut his eyes. In the moment that his eyes were closed, he saw Te Bubas nursing two kittens: one with a spotted back, the other with russet fur like his own. He saw in a flash a battle on a scale he could hardly imagine between two tribes, each with the markings of the first cat's daughters. Thousands of cats fought each other, their blood sinking into the desert sands. Finally he saw his mother rising to speak before a feline assembly. Countless russet-furred cats sat before her, closing their eyes in the greatest display of trust.

Simply speak your self.

My self, thought Mati. He opened his eyes. Mithos was so close now that his rank odor was almost unbearable.

Mithos laughed. "And will you be Mati in death?" he asked. He pressed back onto his haunches, preparing to pounce. A wide grin revealed his pointed teeth, red with the blood of fallen ferals.

"Yes, but it is not my time. I am Mati, son of the last queen of the Abyssinia Tygrine. . . ."

The red smile fell. Mithos's eyes widened.

Within these eyes, a wordless command from the Suzerain far away: "Look away, Mithos! Turn your face, close your eyes!"

Mati heard it, too, although in the cobbled marketplace the ferals heard nothing more than the low wind.

"Mithos!" ordered the Suzerain. *"Turn away! Close your eyes!"*

But Mithos couldn't close his eyes. Moments ago he might have killed the Tygrine cat. But he could not turn away from him now. "Help me, Master!" he shrieked through the dream-wake. "Master? *Master?*"

Mithos's cries echoed through Fiåney, but his master did not reply. The Suzerain had vanished.

Something was happening to Mati. The heat through his paws intensified, his whiskers bristled, and all around him he heard spirits chanting his name, drowning out Mithos's cries.

But Mati's eyes never left Mithos's face.

"I am the last king to inherit the ancient Tygrine throne. I am protector of the third pillar, spirit, of the second self of each and every cat who passes through Fiåney on his journeys between dreams. I am heir to the spirit-queen Te Bubas, the first of our kind. Te Bubas had two daughters, not one: the Sa and the Tygrine, and the spirit of the Tygrine endures through me!" Were Mati's eyes glowing? They felt as though they were on fire.

At last, I know who I am! At last, I make sense! I am the Tygrine cat.

A light brighter than a flame leaped from his eyes as he looked at Mithos. The servant of the Sa gave a defiant yowl and threw back his head, as if struck in the face. In the golden light he became a writhing clot of darkness, a powder of gray dust, then nothing at all. And in less than the blink of an eye, in the space where Mithos had stood, a tiny shoot burst between the cobbles. From the shoot emerged a bud, which unfurled to reveal a perfect golden flower. The flower blossomed for a moment and disappeared.

The world had changed. Jess and the ferals felt it. Cats curled on beds or stalking country gardens felt it, too. The warm, silent glow that lived inside them was safe.

Mati smiled. "A sedicia," he said, exhausted and suddenly joyful.

230

Dawn was rising in the east, touching the cobbled marketplace with a mellow amber light. Jess, the Kanks, and the Cressida Cats drew toward the small ruddy cat. And, one by one, they shut their eyes and stood before the Tygrine King.

Mati was the first to start purring, a small sound in the great world, barely a hum, lost on the early morning breeze. After a few moments, Jess added her high voice to his. Pangur and Sparrow joined in with their rumbling purrs, their eyes remaining shut. Soon, the ferals had all united in this mysterious chorus, purrs high and low, loud and soft, filling the early morning air. The whole world seemed to tremble with their voices. High and low, loud and soft, as constant and endless as the sea.

Epilogue

"Today is a day for celebration," announces Pangur to the Kanks and the Cressida Cats. The ferals have assembled in the park. They aren't afraid of it any more. Pangur stands on a tree stump, the cats encircling him. Cow parsley intrudes upon flower beds, blossom bursts from trees, and everywhere the rich perfume of spring floats through the air. "Today marks the joining of two great kins—the Kanks and the Cressida Cats. As a full moon begins its journey to its highest point, it is my honor to invite the members of the Kanks to join us at Cressida Lock. Homes in the catacombs will be found for all."

The ferals cheer Pangur and each other, reveling in their newfound friendship. The tomcat watches for a moment, tail swishing. Dried blood cakes one of his ears, and as he turns, he limps slightly. But to Mati, standing at a distance,

Pangur is every bit the leader. The experiences of recent weeks and the loss of his brother have changed him. A certainty has set around Pangur's eyes, and there is a strength in his gait. His musk is thick on the evening air.

"It is also a day for mourning the dead," says Pangur. "Six cats fell under Mithos, including my own brave brother, cats who will be remembered in the songs and stories of the ferals for generations."

The cats murmur their agreement, heads raised respectfully, pausing to remember their lost kin. The queens start humming a low lament; the toms fall silent. Mati's whiskers bristle, and he turns his head to peer into the park. Dusk is settling over the flower beds. Rustling between daffodils, Mati senses the second selves of the departed cats, hesitating at the gateway to the shadow world, shifting amid the cow parsley, whispering their good-byes. They merge in the long grass and twist between petals, blending with the air and sinking into the earth.

Mati shuts his eyes. For him, there are others to mourn: his father, whom he never knew, and his mother, who died to protect him. "Amma, where are you?" Mati calls through Fiåney.

He waits for her reassuring purr, but instead he hears only the somber lament of the queens, distant but familiar.

With a twinge of panic, he again calls to his mother: "Amma, please answer me. How will I cope without you? What will I do?"

The lament has all but melted away. The pads of Mati's paws start to tingle, heat rising through them from deep within the earth. Colors spin at the corners of his vision. Vaguely, he recalls how he felt in his earliest days as a kitten—blind, warm, protected. He will remember that feeling: through nights so long that the moon seems to have conquered the sun forever; through winters so cold that summer seems little more than a dream.

A full moon is rising. Mati opens his eyes and looks to the west, where a spring sunset of pinks and reds sinks over the horizon. The tingling from his paws is fading, but the warmth and colors remain. He feels his mother's presence dissolving. She is rising to the land of the spirits, Mati knows, where the souls of cats of exceptional nature live forever.

Mati's mother has left him a gift: his childhood memory. Her forgetting spell has vanished and is replaced by the images, sounds, and smells of Mati's earliest days. At last he remembers his home at the border of the desert, the long winding river where he used to watch waterbirds gather noisily. He remembers scrambling up a pine tree after a large black beetle and not knowing how to get down. Even now, he can almost smell the scent of pine needles and hear the haunting call of turtledoves in the stillness of the midday heat.

He remembers chasing his mother's black-tipped tail and her forgiving smile.

Mati is jolted from his thoughts. Pangur has just addressed

him. The lament has finished. The ferals are staring at Mati with awe and gratitude.

"Mati, please rise and come before the joined kin," says Pangur.

Embarrassed, Mati climbs onto the tree stump next to him. Sparrow sits nearby, a smile animating his large ginger face, joyful and proud. He catches Mati's eye and winks. Mati smiles back gratefully, then turns to Pangur.

Pangur continues. "Mati, you came to our community as a stranger from across the sea. How little we understood who you were, your ancestry, or the special gifts you have at your command. You have demonstrated courage and wisdom beyond your years. While we were distracted in petty local skirmishes, you alone overcame the assassin sent by the Suzerain. You saved us and countless others from a terrible fate!"

"Hear, hear!" cheers Fink.

"Long live Mati!" cries Arabella.

Their praises echo among the ferals. This confuses Mati. Hadn't Fink and Arabella been the first to criticize him, to think the worst? Some cats are just like that, he supposes. He shifts from paw to paw, shrinking from the attention. "I couldn't have done it without help," he mumbles. His eyes wander over the joined kin—over Sparrow, Domino, even Binjax. They come to rest on Jess, who hovers at the edge of the circle, at a distance from the ferals.

Pangur clears his throat. "It is my great honor to bestow

235

on you your full and proper title, your name as decreed by the spirits," he says.

The ferals stiffen, ramrod straight, completely silent. Somewhere, a blackbird is singing.

"*Pirrup*: the Courageous and Sagacious King Mati, Lord of the Tygrine Cats," announces Pangur in a solemn voice.

The ferals stare at Mati with wide, unblinking eyes, even Sparrow and Domino.

The look is unsettling. I'm just the same as I was before, aren't I? Nothing has changed, thinks Mati. For a moment, he remembers facing Mithos, the chanting of spirits, the heat burning from his eyes, the feeling of complete self-belief. Mati can hardly understand where these feelings came from. He is protector of the third pillar, spirit, the second self of every living cat. The weight of this responsibility dawns on him. It is one he will bear for the rest of his life.

Pangur continues: "We hope you will stay with us. This is your home, and we are greatly honored to share it with you. You are our king."

"Thank you," says Mati. He suddenly wants to laugh, but it wouldn't be appropriate. "I will stay. But as just another cat." Pangur starts to protest, but Mati interrupts him. "May I have a word, sir, Mr. Pangur, in private? I have just one request, if that's OK. . . ."

"But, Sire, the meeting is in session," starts the black tom, glancing around uneasily, and Mati has the feeling that he's failed to follow their rules. Pangur catches himself. This is no longer just a catling he's addressing—it is, after all, the King of the Tygrine Cats, and a cat of unrivaled power. "Sorry, my lord—is it something pressing?"

"It is," agrees Mati.

Pangur nods, turning to the joined kin. "Friends, you will forgive me and King Mati if we leave you for a while."

They walk a short distance away from the kin.

"Pangur, sir," begins Mati.

"Sire, you should not be addressing me as 'sir'—it's not right!" exclaims Pangur.

Mati glances back at the ferals, and at the small tortoise-shell-and-white cat with the red collar who sits washing herself several tail lengths away from the others. He is impatient to continue. "Pangur, I would like to talk to you about Jess. . . ."

"I'm sure the hinds will try to pull up the dandelions and cow parsley by the roots. They think they're weeds. They only like tulips and roses," says Trillion.

"I'm sure they will. But they'll be fighting a losing battle. We ferals are like weeds, in a way," chuckles Sparrow.

The cats sit around him, exchanging confused glances. "How's that, Sparrow?" asks Torko, a Kank.

"Well, aren't we part domestic, part wild? Bursting up in cities wherever there's space. We can't be trodden down. And they'll never get rid of us!"

The cats laugh in agreement.

237

Mati is sitting alone in the place where Etheleldra's oak once stood, remembering the spirit Bayo, remembering his mother. Jess approaches to sit beside him. Mati hears her tinkling bell even before he sees her. She is the only one who is not shy of him, treating him as she always has, as a friend rather than as royalty. She's the one who gave him the tour of the marketplace soon after his arrival, who stood up for him when the others thought the worst—who returned when she realized that he was in danger.

"Pangur has invited me to stay, properly this time," says Jess. "I can move into the catacombs, have my own chamber there. He says the collar can be cut, that I'll be free."

"Hooray!" cries Mati. "We'll be friends forever and ever!"
He doesn't tell her about his chat with Pangur.

"Yes."

Something in her tone makes Mati turn to look at her more closely. Barely detectable, there's a trace of sorrow. "You want to stay, don't you?" he asks.

"Of course!" says Jess.

He watches her. Suddenly, he remembers the visit of her old man to the marketplace. He remembers how hard the man had searched for her, how willingly Jess had left with him. She had been happy, he realizes.

He thinks of the Jess he had known before. Always lost. What had she said? "Home is a feeling."

Mati looks to the west. The sun has already danced past the moon. Soon it will have sunk beyond the horizon.

Amma, what should I do? he wonders.

A gentle evening wind presses back Mati's whiskers. Nearby, he hears the Cressida and Kank kins exchanging stories, like long-lost friends reunited. Sparrow is entertaining them with a fable about sardines. An ache grows in Mati's chest. For a moment he turns back to Jess, who is watching him closely. He glances beyond her toward the river. He remembers the words of the spirit Bayo: "She who is lost must not remain so forever."

Mati reaches past the growing ache in his chest, finds the word he needs: "Go."

Jess pauses before she speaks. Her eyes widen. "Mati, I won't—"

"You must go," he says decisively. "You own, Jess. That is a great responsibility. Your hind, this old hind of yours, has become attached to you. He cannot do without you." The words scratch Mati's throat, but he continues. "He is waiting for you, Jess. He won't understand. How can you expect a hind to understand the ways of cats? He'll think you've abandoned him. He'll think you don't love him." Here, Mati allows himself a quick glance in Jess's direction. Their eyes meet, and Mati's throat tightens.

Tell her to stay, his every sense urges him. *Beg her to stay!*

Mati falls silent, no longer trusting his voice to say the right words. Jess is watching him with her huge green eyes. He sees sadness there but also hope. He tries to remember how she looks right now, the pretty patchwork of her tortoiseshell face. *Will this image fade too?* he wonders. He draws it toward him, toward his second self, protecting it from the passage of time. Here among his memories, Jess will remain like this forever.

Finally she speaks. "I would have stayed if you'd asked me."

"I know," says Mati. "Do you know the way back?"

"Yes," purrs Jess. She steps toward him, presses her muzzle against his cheek. Mati shuts his eyes. "Stay safe, for all of us, my friend," she whispers. Then she turns from him at a run, sprinting past the resting ferals, beyond the borders of the park, into another world.

Mati sits quietly for a moment. And then he does something extraordinary. Something that only one cat has done before him. He cries, two tears, which roll down his cheeks and catch on his whiskers.

"Mati, sir? Lord—that is, King Mati?" Domino approaches nervously.

Mati wipes his eyes with a russet paw. "Please, just 'Mati.'" He remembers the words of the spirit Bayo: "The one you doubt has loyalty that you cannot see. He believes in you."

At the time, Mati didn't know to whom this referred. Now he realizes. "Thank you, Domino," he says.

The little harlequin catling looks surprised. He's about to speak, but Pangur has arrived. Domino nods and steps away, leaving Pangur and Mati alone. Mati will catch up with him later. Tonight they will leap together at invisible

mice through rustling cow parsley. They will be friends for
life.

"*Pirrup*: the Courageous and Sagacious King Mati, Lord
of the Tygrine Cats," begins Pangur, "the moon is at its highest point; your kin awaits you." The other cats are out of
earshot. Pangur glances over his shoulder, lowers his eyes.
He starts to say something else, then hesitates. When
he speaks, it is barely a whisper. "My lord . . . I wanted to
say . . . to say sorry . . ."

Again, the words of the spirit Bayo return to Mati: "There
is another. Do not judge him too harshly. He is young, and
although his heart his good, his courage will fail him."

The chief had made mistakes. But hadn't they all? In the
end, he had acted bravely. And Etheleldra was right.
Judgment, the second pillar, was important, but it should be
used with great caution. What had she said? "We are all of
flesh and fur."

"It's all right," says Mati.

It isn't much, but Pangur glances up gratefully. "Leadership of the joined kin is yours," he says.

Mati is watching him steadily. He shakes his head. "I
won't take it. You're a natural leader, Pangur, and we're safe
with you."

"Those least drawn to power are often the best placed to
take it," says Pangur.

Someone has said that to Mati before. He tries to remember.

Pangur smiles. "One day, when you're a little older, I have a feeling you will lead this kin to finer things. We shall see, my lord."

Mati smiles too. His new title still embarrasses him. "Please," he says, "just Mati."

Dawn breaks over the city: eager shafts of sunlight probe between houses, reach into windows. The old man is mumbling in his sleep. A band of light escapes between the curtains to hover over his bed. A faint noise downstairs wakens him. His hand instinctively moves to the side of the bed where his cat always curls.

Instead of fur, his fingers touch the cotton sheets, cold against his skin. Then he remembers. "Jess," he sighs. "My dear Jess." In spite of himself, his eyes fill with tears. "Nothing but an old fool," he murmurs. He presses his fingers against his eyes.

The bedroom door creaks, and suddenly the old man hears the tinkling of a bell, feels silky fur against his hand. His eyes open.

A small tortoiseshell-and-white cat stands before him. *I'm back now,* she purrs. *I'm back for good.*

The old man strokes her head gently. "Jess, dear Jess," he whispers. "I knew you'd come home."